PRAISE
ANGEL DUST

"Admirably devious, laugh-out-loud sick, and shockingly smart, Jeremy Robert Johnson blew me away with *Angel Dust Apocalypse*. Johnson's verve for the surreal is high-octane: he burrows down deep into the twisted pathologies of his characters with the reckless abandon of a greased pig squealing down the pipings of a carnival slide. His writing is ferocious and fearless...and though it reminded me of a whole school of dark visionaries, it's truly in a league all its own. It's been awhile since I read something that actually made me do a double take, but this book had me reading passages over and over again, marveling over the ingenuity, chuckling over the inventiveness, and standing in awe of the sheer guts it takes to write like this. *Angel Dust Apocalypse* is a dark, imaginative treasure — sophisticated, disturbing, witty, and refreshingly twisted. Surrealist horror — absurdist excess — and pure postmodern fun. You absolutely must read this book right away. It'll change you in a way you couldn't imagine."
— Michael A. Arnzen, author of *100 Jolts* and *Play Dead*

"Jeremy Robert Johnson's one of the freshest, weirdest writers out there right now, and he's just getting started."
—Alan M. Clark, author/illustrator of *The Paint in My Blood*

"In one inky scream Jeremy Robert Johnson has established himself as a virtuoso counterculture voice that must be heard. Listen to his siren song with bleeding ears and smile like a lipless wonder, like a marathon masturbator, like a sentient plague. You are guaranteed to enjoy this finely orchestrated literary Armageddon."
—John Edward Lawson, author of *Last Burn in Hell*

ANGEL DUST
APOCALYPSE

JEREMY ROBERT JOHNSON

ERASERHEAD PRESS
PORTLAND, OR

ERASERHEAD PRESS
205 NE BRYANT
PORTLAND, OR 97211

WWW.ERASERHEADPRESS.COM

ISBN: 0-9762498-3-9

"League of Zeroes" originally appeared in *Verbicide #11*. "Dissociative Skills" originally appeared in *City Slab #6*. "Amniotic Shock in the Last Sacred Place" originally appeared in *Pain and Other Petty Plots to Keep You in Stitches* (IFD Publishing). "Snowfall" originally appeared in *Verbicide #13*. "Working at Home" originally appeared in *THE EDGE: Tales of Suspense #18*. "Luminary" originally appeared in *Darker Than Tin, Brighter Than Sin* (Rabe Phillips, Ed.) "Sparklers Burning" originally appeared at HORRORFIND: Fiction. "Wall of Sound: A Movement in Three Parts" originally appeared as "Liquidation" in *Happy #15*, "Deeper" in *Glass Tesseract Vol. #3*, and "A Number of Things Come to Mind" in *Happy #17*.

Printed in the USA.

ACKNOWLEDGEMENTS

(A Huge) Thank you to CM3 and Rose at Eraserhead Press/Avant Punk.

Thank you to the following Oregon writers for their wisdom and encouragement:

Nina K. Hoffman, Elizabeth Engstrom, Alan M. Clark, Bruce Holland Rogers, and Chuck Palahniuk.

Thank you to the following musical artists. These stories were written under the influence:

The Mars Volta, Glassjaw, El-P, The Roots, Home Before Sundown, Saul Williams, Massive Attack, Civ, and DJ Dieselboy.

TABLE OF CONTENTS

DEDICATION

To Rand, Selby, Wallace, Burroughs, Vonnegut, Welsh, Williams, Palahniuk, Barker, King, and Ellroy-

For showing me what words can do.

THE LEAGUE OF ZEROES

It's obvious she's having a hard time sipping her coffee. No matter how delicately she raises her hand or how straight and elegant her posture, she can't help looking awkward when she drinks. Half the damn cup of coffee is trickling its way to the spreading brown stain on the front of her white blouse.

It's her fault, really. She's the one that wanted to have her lips removed.

She'll adapt. We all do.

She'll figure out how to keep her gums moisturized with Vaseline, and she'll carry a small container of it in her purse at all times.

She'll learn to drink with a straw tucked into the side of her cheek. You can still get some good suction like that and the method cuts the mess to nothing.

She'll get her teeth bonded and bleached to emphasize their newfound prominence.

She'll figure out how to make plosive sounds with her tongue against the back of her gums.

She'll be looking good and find it even easier to smile.

I think she's gorgeous, sans shirtfront stain, but I don't think she'd go for a guy like me. I consider crossing the coffee shop and trying a pick-up line, but the three prongs I've had my tongue split into feel swollen and tied up. Still healing, I guess.

She might find my iris-free eyes attractive. They're all pupil; very black, mysterious and hard to read. That might work for her.

Deep down inside, I know she'd never go for an amateur freak like me. She's the type of elegant, slightly-modified trophy girl-friend I see hanging around with Body Modification Royalty.

I'll save myself the embarrassment for now. Once I join the League of Zeroes, though, she's mine.

The thought of being a freak show all-star brings my all-black eyes back to my sketchbook. I'm looking at the drawing of my body mod design, wondering just how the hell my brain is going to look outside of my body. I hope it's symmetrical. I've never had to worry about brain aesthetics until I came up with my plan.

I want to detach my brain from my body. I want to polish it up and put it in a nice display case and carry it around with me, like a sidekick.

My Buddy the Brain.

I jot notes around the sketch.

How do I keep the brain clean and presentable?

What kind of fiber-optics can transmit neuro-signals to my spinal cord?

How do I do this and not die?

Is it worth it?

I look up and across the room at Our Lady of Liplessness. I picture her licking the box I will keep my brain in, loving my presence, asking me what it's like to be in the League of Zeroes.

She'll think I'm special.

It's worth it.

I wonder for a moment longer about asking her for a date, see if she wants to check out the Italian Horror Movie Festival on Fifteenth. I pass on the idea. Maybe it's just sublimated embarrass-ment, but she looks a little uptight. She might bite.

I head out of the coffee shop and kick over three blocks in

the cold until I get to a telephone booth. I sweep the coin return for change and come back with a finger load of ketchup. At least I hope that it's ketchup. I'm curious, but I skip the smell and taste test and smear the red goop on the glass of the phone booth wall in front of me. I drop in some coins, press seven buttons.

Raymond picks up the phone on the other end and says, "SaladMan here!"

The second I hear his voice I feel like I wasted eighty-five cents.

"Hey, Ray, it's Jamie. Cool it on the SaladMan shit, you don't have to market to me."

"I know, Jamie, I'm just trying to stay on point. I'm picking up a lot of regional buzz and a couple of the BMR's have mentioned me on the website."

Ray, who is my best friend based only on our mutual lack of total resentment, is obsessed with joining the upper echelon of the League of Zeroes. He keeps talking.

"I'm serious, Jamie. I'm like days from becoming Body Modification Royalty myself. You know Aggie WoodSpine? He's always putting in a good word for me on the circuit, and Marshall Le Crawl has said, and I'm almost quoting like verbatim here, that I have one of the most original modification schemes he's ever seen. That's on the damn website."

"I know, Ray, I'm aware of the accolades. I'm not doubting you. I've got more pressing business at hand, that's all, so if I seem impatient it's only because what you're saying isn't important."

"Thanks, Jamie. What's going on?"

"Meet me at the Italian Horror Movie Festival in twenty minutes, okay. We'll check out some Fulci, watch some eyeballs burst, and then we'll go get coffee and I'll tell you about my new scheme. I think I've come up with something really special."

"Cool, I'll catch you later."

"Oh, hey Salad…hey Ray."

"Yeah."

"I saw another chick with no lips today. I think that style's about to blow up."

"Yeah. I've seen that around lately. How'd she look?"

"Pretty sharp, man. Pretty sharp."

We're heading out of the theater halfway through the movie 'cause we've already seen the best stuff; the scene where that kid gets the drill through his skull all slow, and the one where that demon priest sucks out that girl's organs just by staring at her.

Ray and I are walking in the flickering light of the faded theater marquee and I'm anxious, hoping for something more visceral in my life. No more celluloid thrills and vicarious rendering of the flesh. I'm ready for my next surgery and I can't wait to tell Ray my plans.

I pop in to a Super Saver Mart while Ray waits out front. It costs me thirty bucks for a pack of Marlboro Chronics, a soda, two Charleston Chews, and a dropper of Visine. Half of the money goes to taxes. I have to give the government credit for that one. The same day they legalized weed they went and imposed a sin tax on candy and eye drops. It's almost devious enough to be admirable.

We head over to D. Brewster's Café and find some plush seats far from the speakers where we can have a conversation. I don't order anything because I've already got my soda and chocolate, and Ray picks up an extra large mocha.

Ray is starting to smell. I think some of his vegetables have gone south again, even though Dr. Tikoshi soaked them in preservative this time. The lettuce sewn into his neck looks like it's browning at the edges, and the tip of the carrot emerging unicorn proud from his forehead has broken off. The sutures around the radish spliced into his right forearm look swollen and irritated.

Right from the beginning I told him SaladMan was a screwed-up scheme. I told him that perishables were always too high maintenance. He's right about the attention he's garnering though; even now people are staring at him. Still, on a purely olfactory level spending time with Ray is like hanging out with a big pile of compost.

Despite his odor, he gets big points for ambition. He's got some respectable friends on the circuit and if he can get someone to endorse him as Body Modification Royalty he can do some tour time and then apply for the League of Zeroes.

The League. It's the big money, the endorsements, the adulation, the weekly primetime broadcasts, and the outright worship of the people.

Ray's got his goals set high. If he makes it big he'll be able to buy fresh produce every day, and eventually he'll be able to afford that platinum dressing decanter that he wants to have installed in his ribcage.

I've got him beat though. After my next modification I'll be an indelible image in the public eye. My plan is the fourth ace that nobody thought I had.

I lean in through a cloud of thick smoke and start to whisper my scheme into SaladMan's cauliflowered right ear.

I'm alone and walking home with my thin jean jacket wrapped tight around my shoulders.

I hear Ray's voice in the café whispering, "Jamie, that's *impossible*. What makes you think you could live through that kind of modification?"

I try to brush his comment off, but his concern sounded genuine. I try not to take it to heart. I'm so excited about my imminent fame that mortality has become a second-string worry.

Maybe Ray's just jealous.

I shake Ray's doubts out of my head and remember how great my scheme is. It's worth the gamble. I've never been one to swallow motivational speaker pablum but I've always nodded in agreement at the phrase, "You've got to play big to win big!" So, I'm choosing not to acknowledge the danger. Now entering Ostrich Mode, head firmly inserted in sand.

On my way home I walk past trashcan fires and drug deals and I hear sirens wailing and glass breaking and a bag lady nearby mumbles something about wires embedded in the Earth telling all of us what to do.

A League of Zeroes poster stapled to a telephone pole advertises an upcoming appearance by S. O. Faygus and his amazing translucent throat.

An ad beneath the poster promises a two-for-one deal on mail-order brides.

Another asks me if I really trust my gas mask.

It all leaves me with the impression that I'm living in some kind of ravaged nuclear wasteland. The problem with that diagnosis lies in the absence of any level of apocalypse. No one dropped any bombs; no great fire scorched the Earth.

We just ended up like this. We followed a natural progression from past to present. We're not Post-Apocalyptic, we're Post-Yesterday.

One look around, though, and I realize that we must have had some brutal kind of Yesterday.

Ray's voice is still in my head, echoing doubt, stirring up stomach acid.

"Jamie, that's impossible!"

It can't be.

This plan is all I have. It's my only chance of getting off these streets.

It's the only way I'll ever be special.

Dr. Tikoshi wouldn't take me on as a patient.

Dr. Komatsu had me ejected from his building.

I had to go to my old standby, Dr. Shinori. He's the only one who likes to experiment. He's the only one willing to push boundaries. He's the only one that would take a credit card.

I'm moments from anesthesia and Dr. Shinori is sharpening his diamond bone saw. He has emphasized several times how difficult this will be. He hasn't said anything, and I wouldn't understand a single word he'd say, but we've been communicating with drawings.

I showed him a picture of my design, the new me, the guaranteed League of Zeroes member.

He sketched for a moment and showed me a picture. On the left there was a big, bright smiley face, and on the right there was a little stick figure drawing of my body resting in a casket.

I hope this means my chances are fifty/fifty.

I suspect this might mean he'd be happy to kill me. He gets my money either way. I signed the Goddamn waiver. I'm taking the dive.

I go over the reasons in my head, even though it's too late to turn back. People would assume I take the risks and bear the public scrutiny because there's money in it. They wouldn't be totally wrong. The freak show industry pulls in millions every year, and gets more lucrative as time passes. More fame, more attention. Those things don't hurt. Before I started this, before I split my tongue into three prongs and had my irises removed and my toes extended, I was dirt poor and always felt like I was ugly anyway. Now I'm so ugly that people can't look away, *and* I can pull advertising dollars.

The number one reason I do this? People jump to assumptions and whisper asides to each other about parental neglect or abuse or acid in my baby formula. They're wrong.

I do this because when I was little my mom told me I was going to be someone *special*.

I asked her what special meant. She pointed to the TV screen. I thought "special" was Burt Reynolds, until she spoke up.

"Special means that people pay attention to you. Special means you have something that other people don't. Special is having people love you without even knowing you. I know, and have known since the day you were born, that you are going to be special. That's why I love you so much, Jamie."

So, I waited to become special.

By the time I hit twenty, I was just like everyone else.

I still am.

Which is not to say that I'm Mr. Free Spirit Railing Against Conformity, because everyone else does *that* too. I just know that I'm not special, and I have to force the change.

Mom calls me less and less these days.

The hugs are shorter than they used to be.

So here I am, a product of forcible evolution trying to stay one step ahead of the other mutants, hoping my mommy pays attention.

Dr. Shinori puts the gas mask over my mouth and nose and doesn't ask me to start counting backwards from a hundred. I know the routine. By ninety-five I'm floating in a soft yellow ocean made from rose petals. Somewhere further away I'm shaking as the bone saw hits meat.

The stage lights are especially bright tonight, but I can still make out the audience. The women with no lips always look pleased, grinning wide as the valley.

Ray is in the front row tonight. I flew him out here, even though he's Body Modification Royalty now and could afford it himself. He's not wearing a shirt and the baby tomatoes sewn into his chest spell out SaladMan, which is pretty sound promotion.

As the leader of the League of Zeroes I get to make a closing address to our national audience each Thursday.

My mom is in the audience, like always, and I'm planning a great address tonight, something about how Love Evolves Us All.

They'll eat it up, but they won't understand the costs that come with being truly *special*. They won't know about the white-fire headaches. They won't know about the pressure that shoots down my spine when I change the oxygenated cerebrospinal fluid. They won't know what it's like when your brain signals get backed up and a dream hits you while your eyes are wide open. I keep these things to myself. I don't even tell my mom. She thinks I'm perfect now.

The audience always likes to hear about how I'm doing, first thing in the show. I tell them my brain is getting a little hot under these stage lights and that gets a good, hearty laugh. I'm laughing with them, but inside I'm genuinely concerned and I shift my hands to the left and try to move the clear, titanium-laced plastic box I keep my brain in towards the shadows. It tugs on the fiber optic lines running into my neck at the top of my spinal cord, but I manage.

I adapt. We all do.

DISSOCIATIVE SKILLS

Curt Lawson felt like a surgeon right up until the moment he snorted the horse tranquilizer. He sniffed hard and then raised his head to survey the scalpel/gauze/suture kit layout on the ratty, orange, shag carpet next to him. His vinyl bean-bag crinkled beneath him as he sat upright and set down his powder-dusted vanity mirror.

The digital clock across the room confirmed that he had three hours before Mom and Dad would be back from their ballroom dancing class.

"Dance away, little parents." Curt spoke the words slowly in his empty, Spartan bedroom and received no response. Curt's face became Artic-cold numb, and he looked around his room through the new eyes the Ketamine had given him.

The previously drab white walls and wooden clothes closet now seemed sleek and stylish. His weathered, hand-me-down couch began to look like a plush boat. The empty space between Curt's bean-bag residence and his thin mattress across the room became desert-wide and arid. The normally shabby shag carpet beneath his bare feet took on a new, puppy dog softness, and he clenched it in his numbing toes.

The brutal rubberband flavored drip and paint thinner burn in his sinuses sent his brain back to his powder purchase earlier that day.

He'd found his dealer, Dave "The Wave" D'Amato, by the soda machine outside the drama room at Shelton High. Dave had been wearing a plain blue jumpsuit and a tan backpack.

"Parachuting later today?" Curt had asked.

Dave had smiled, a split second smile that faded away fast enough to let Curt know his medicine man wasn't in a joking mood. "No, I'm afraid of heights, Curt. What do you need?"

"Well, I missed breakfast this morning and I was wondering if you happened to have some Special K."

Dave gave the short smile again, all business.

"Yeah, Curt, I got some K, but it's on some heavy Ketalar pharmy level shit, and it's been cut with some diazepam for your blood pressure."

"My blood pressure, Dave?"

"Yeah, dog, without that diazepam in there the K would make your veins all bulge out and your eyes would feel like they was going to pop. Also, this shit burns black super-quick, so it's got some kind of speed, probably benzedrine, or something, up in it."

"Is that bad?"

"Naw, dog, it's all right 'cause *that* shit'll keep your heart beating even when the ketamine's telling it to stop. So it's actually a bonus. And, of course, there's probably some GKWE in there."

"GKWE?"

"Yup, GKWE. That's some God Knows What Else. By the time I get my shit it's been through more hands than I even know. And everybody cuts it a little. Everybody."

Dave wasn't a comforting drug dealer, but he was a straight shooter. Curt had never known another 16-year-old as honest. Or as driven. The kid put half his crooked income into a savings account for his eventual med school tuition.

A Portrait of the Anesthesiologist as a Young Man.

Back in the narcotic now Curt laughed to himself, bowed his head back to the beckoning yellow lines, and snorted another rail of K. He inhaled deep and a lungful of stale bedroom air chased the powder up the straw.

Curt leaned back in his bean-bag and let the straw drop from his nose onto his chest. The world went slow motion and the air got souped-up, thick with gravity.

"Am I breathing?" Curt wondered.

He tried to hold a hand up in front of his mouth to check for exhalation. His hand had other ideas and remained inert. The ketamine staple gun had him pinned as he lay.

Motion, for the moment, was a non-option.

Curt's first thought was panic heavy. "What if I drop into a K-hole? If I go zombie right away then I can't use the scalpel."

Reason launched a sneak attack. "This is just the first wave of the high. Let it crest and then get to work. For the meantime, *feel this*."

His reptile brain locked into the chemical vibe, and his cortex began to sizzle with bad electricity. Curt uttered a low "Gwaaaaah" as his eyes rolled back and began to twitch, blurring the rainbow spectrum of light provided by the string of Christmas bulbs circling the ceiling of his room.

His brain did the wrong things he'd hoped it would do.

Sound came into his system wrong. The classical music from his cheap plastic boom-box became tiny sonic wasps with sharp violin stingers. They buzzed around his head, a soundswarm that penetrated his ears and nose and mouth and injected him with disjointed musical notes until his skin shivered. Horns like repressed peasants moaning slow. Wrong.

The distance between Curt's head and the surrounding walls fluctuated from fingernail-thin to epic-black-space wide.

He could smell the old sweat and dried semen on his bedding across the room. It was a human smell and made him feel small and weak for a moment. "Maybe I shouldn't be doing this. Maybe I should call the hospital or Mom's cell phone or…"

The thought was cut off by another wave of anesthetic bliss.

Then the air of his spare, stale room became amniotic and warm and safe, except for his moments of mental alarm.

Curt found himself thinking, with nagging frequency, "Am I

breathing?" The question was easily written off once he noticed the tiny faces that lived in the wood-grain doors of his clothes closet.

The faces laughed, growled, knew Curt and smiled at him, grew bodies, fought, fucked, killed. It was a tip-top hallucination. Curt could barely look away until he realized that he had sat upright and could now move his limbs.

He inhaled deep as he regained some level of physical control. He was not surprised when he smelled French fries, and realized that he had vomited his dinner onto his shirt.

The shirt was easily discarded. It had to go anyway. Curt needed access to the soft skin of his belly.

Curt reached over to the scalpel laid out by the bean-bag and managed to wrap his left hand around it.

"I thought I'd have a little more control than this. I'll have to be extra careful. I can do this. I MUST DO THIS."

His yell echoed against the plaster walls of the room. The faces in the wood-grain recoiled at the sound.

"Sorry, guys. I just, well, I need to do this sort of thing."

He knew the little faces understood.

Every *wrong* thing done was a show of strength. An exercise in control. Proof that life could be contained and managed, down to the tiniest, strangest detail, if only for a moment.

"You know that. Right, little faces?"

A twisted wood-whorl face winked at Curt and confirmed the understanding. The liquid wood grain folks knew the secret score. They knew that with every wrong thing Curt did, he was separating himself from the predictable degradation of his gin-guzzling, Prozac-popping parents, from the random humanity of bad skin and poorly timed bowel movements, from the After School Special cliché of his generation's own pre-packaged rebellion. The things Curt did were special, completely unique in their own way.

"I'm different," Curt told himself.

Past exercises in control had been successful. Curt would think something, and if the next immediate thought was, "Well, I could never do that." then he'd do it, whatever he'd thought, no matter how wrong. That was the litmus and the litany.

Curt knew how long it took to eat a pound of Crisco. He knew the nervous sweat that preceded smashing his own thumb with a hammer. He knew what it was like to go to a party in a wheelchair, wearing a Skynnrd t-shirt, asking girls if they wanted to "rollerfuck his freebird." He knew the discomfort of spending an entire day with a travel toothbrush jammed up his ass. He knew what it was like to kill a fly, eat half of it, and deposit the remaining thorax and twitching wing into his left ear.

Sometimes he felt as if he was training towards a gold medal in the Dumbfuck Olympics. Sometimes he felt wonderful, like his acts, however bizarre, were taking him closer to some kind of greatness. He constantly reassured himself.

"No one else has ever done this. You are the only one strong enough to make it happen." He stood proud and walked head high amongst the living dead, a man in control of his future, tossing fate aside.

Even his pain was unique. He sought it out and cultivated its strangeness. It trumped the boring pains of the everyday world. The bright burn that shot through his system while gouging his tonsils with a chopstick made his boring, human migraines seem lukewarm.

"Pre-emptive suffering makes me stronger," he'd often thought to himself.

Curt's secret-subversive diet burned holes in his stomach lining. His belly never stopped grumbling. Indigestion was his constant companion. He wanted to re-write that "footsteps on the beach" poem and replace Jesus with indigestion.

So he did. The last line had read, "That was when I gurgled you."

The experiments in control always had their harbingers. The Crisco-eating incident was set in motion by an embarrassing, in-class sneeze that had very publicly layered his hands with mucous. The toothbrush colonoscopy was predated by an uncontrollable erection Curt had failed to hide from his teacher in gym class.

Yesterday, Curt had sat down to breakfast with his parents.

His dad's hands had trembled until he popped the top of his breakfast beer. Curt's mother had noted this and laughed, a dry, quiet laugh that reeked of acceptance. Her laugh seemed to Curt like the sound of a zoo animal finding the humor in its cage.

Curt fell asleep crying that night, unable to tear his mind away from his father's softly shaking hands and the sound of his mother's laugh, hating the dime-store pathos of the moment, hating himself for not being able to distance himself from it.

This morning he'd awakened to the thought, "I'll never know what I look like inside."

So Curt followed his own rules, copped the K, and borrowed the scalpel that now sat centimeters from his belly.

Curt delayed his self-surgery for a second, remembering to sterilize the instrument. The butane from his lighter heated the blade and seared carbon black on the silver surface.

He paused for a moment and pinched his face, which he had a hard time locating. Once he got a large chunk of cheek between his forefinger and thumb he squeezed as hard as he could.

He felt nothing. No skin against skin, only a dull pressure.

Perfect. Numb. Time to operate. Time to tour the belly.

His right hand shook but steadied as the scalpel met resistance. The wood faces flinched as the blade separated skin without a sound.

Curt hadn't imagined there would be so much blood. He hadn't planned on the mesentery tissue being so tenacious, even under the honed edge of the scalpel. He'd also thought that the small intestine would be, well, small. The three inches of tubing that he'd managed to pull through the incision were wider than two of his fingers side-by-side.

Curt stared at the bit of his insides that he'd excavated. He listened to the stream of orchestral music coming from his stereo and wondered if Amadeus had ever had the willpower to expose his own insides.

Curt seriously doubted it. He looked at his achievement with love and softly stroked the moist, red bit of intestine that jutted from his bleeding belly. He stared and watched the previously unknowable part of him shimmering in the colored Christmas lights.

"I am in control. I made this happen. I own my life," he thought.

A tiny twinge of pain crept into the invaded area after a few minutes of intense observation.

"The ketamine's starting to wear off," Curt thought.

This thought was preceded in his mind by the sound of the front door opening and then closing.

"Oh, God. Mom and Dad are home."

The knock on the door to his room came too quickly and sounded wrecking-ball heavy. He tried to speak; he wanted to say, "Stay out, I'm naked."

The ketamine might as well have removed his tongue and wired his jaw shut. Total disconnect had set in.

His mother opened the door.

She stared and then shook her head as if to throw the image of her son from the surface of her eyes.

Then she screamed, the high, operatic shriek of a woman confronting something which cannot be real, something *wrong*. Curt could smell the vodka on her breath from across the room.

It was a nice, warm smell, and it stayed printed on his senses all the way to the hospital, a sensory presence hijacking a spot in his mind. It was the scent of her scream. It was proof that he'd done something incredible, something the world and *certainly* his mother had never seen.

Her vodka-soaked shriek was a trophy. It was the first real, intense emotion he'd heard from his medicated mother in a long time. The sound betrayed the smooth, idle complacency of her everyday life.

He wished that he could have spoken to her. He had wanted to say, "Try to accept this. Laugh at *this*, Mom."

Even his father had been shocked sober, and jumped into action. Dad's hands had held steady while trying in vain to push Curt's intestine back into place.

For just a moment, Curt's exercise in control had enveloped his whole family, and brought them together. He'd forced them to abandon their slow, slaughterhouse fattening for a moment and really live, and fight.

Had they slipped into drunken slumber without first checking in on him, Curt imagined he'd still be bleeding, numb, watching himself die in the Technicolor glow of his Christmas lights.

But they'd fought.

His parents had both held him, one at each side, until the ambulance showed up. Their hands had been clenched together over his belly, staunching the warm flow of his blood.

Though he couldn't move his limbs or say a word during the ambulance ride, Curt began to feel again, and his own screams found their way into the world.

Despite the fire in his belly, beneath his wounded-animal bellowing, he felt proud.

Inside, and out.

AMNIOTIC SHOCK IN THE LAST SACRED PLACE

The drugs were wearing off. James Toddle's mind slowly broke the surface of the soft purple ocean that had engulfed it. Consciousness crept back into his skull and threw its weight around, asserting its ugly but undeniable presence.

He felt straps pinning him to a cold metal table. He felt the persistent travel of insects across his skin. He felt reality setting in.

Reality was the last thing he wanted. Reality told him he was a grown man wearing a giant diaper. Reality told him he had a nasty habit of hurting the women he so desperately desired love from. Reality was adult judgments and adult institutions and adult terms like "pathological need" and "infantilism." Reality was a place where his need and his hunger were becoming harder and harder to satiate.

James became so mired in self pity he didn't even notice the pervasive slaughterhouse smell that saturated the air around him. The sickness of his surroundings meant little next to his loneliness and ever present need for love and attention.

He was weeping crocodile tears onto pudgy pink cheeks when the dope tube descended from the ceiling. He felt the metal nozzle slide between his lips and pump his mouth full of chemicals and protein pulp. Instinctively, he began to nurse.

Soon he was sleeping like a newborn baby, calm as a lamb despite the shrieks and wet screams and locust swarms of laughter that echoed throughout the Facility. His lips were wrapped leech-tight around the rusted metal nozzle that fed him and filled his body with pain-killer and his mind with fever dreams. The dream was almost always the same and had been since he could remember. He was small again and he was being held tight and kept warm because he was special. A cuter, more wondrous child had never been born. He was feeding and he could close his eyes and feel his mother's love flowing over him, and into him, through her soft milk. Eventually, though, the feeding stopped, and he was still hungry. *So hungry.* He wanted more milk, more love, more attention. He bit down harder on the breast in his mouth. He clamped down until he felt flesh separate and a chunk of his mother was in his belly and then he felt something flowing, something hot and salty, and he swallowed deep and hoped it would never end.

It was the crinkling of the plastic diaper that gave her hope. Nurse Sebac turned towards the sound that echoed in the oily ear puddles on each side of her head. Her optic nerves, long since exposed by an accidental Procedure Frenzy, wiggled in the air before her face, and pulled in her sight like an extended snake's tongue would pull in smell.

A vision of loveliness lay there before her, held to the floating storage table by thin straps of what appeared to be rhino hide. She twitched nervously for a second, looking around the room, wondering if it was possible to be attacked by a skinned rhino twice in one week. "Bad odds," she whispered to herself, trying to remain calm enough to study the patient.

There on the table, wearing only an oversized plastic diaper, and smelling heavily of talcum powder, was one of the shiniest, softest men she'd ever seen. A cracked and leaking tube hung down from the ceiling and ended in the patient's mouth. He was suckling at it, his lips pulling a combination of benzerol and somnambuline into his throat.

Nurse Sebac stamped the bony heel of her foot into the fleshy, ovular Pad that glowed yellow in front of the patient's storage table. The Pad squeaked, glowed brighter yellow, and slimed away, leaving a shiny trail on the shattered formica flooring beneath it. It slithered back a minute later with a clipboard stuck to its top. She lifted the clipboard from the Pad and then kicked the glowing yellow globule across the room, where it sunk into the wall, whinnying as it dissipated.

She read the patient profile, which was written backwards and contained the words "parquet", "luggage", and "immolation." The one important piece of information was located on the back of the profile sheet, spelled out with pink crayon. Below the heading marked "Your Name:" it read "James Toddle."

She would need to know his name when he woke up in her hidden apartment, high in the upper floors of the Facility. She would need to know what to call the man in the giant diaper before the procedure could begin.

Nurse Sebac dragged James Toddle behind her, making sure to let his table bump into the shifting walls around her. She had removed his tubes and hoped that the lack of anesthetic and constant jostling would wake him by the time they reached her secluded Facility hideaway in the swaying upper reaches. She passed by Crew members and staff during her ascension. Any questions about her movement of the patient were covered with a pre-fabricated lie.

"Backscatter has requested that I saturate this man with various waste products and then oil him up and set him out on Veranda 8."

At that point everyone who stopped her would ask the same question, to which she would respond, "Yes, that's where we're keeping the razor-beaked turtles these days."

It seemed reasonable.

She continued up flight after flight of sticky stairs, and thought about her new project. Nurse Sebac had to have her hobbies, like any other victim of the nine to five to three to nine workdays. "Hobbies keep you sane," she told herself.

"So I take a few patients here and there, what's the harm? It's not like a big Facility like this is going to miss a few piddling, worthless patients, what with the thousands they process every day. *Especially* after they cut my morphine back to the daily bucket, it's like they owe *me*. I'm doing them a favor and keeping this place running more efficiently. They should thank me for working my fingers to the bone. In fact, this is my third set of hands this year!"

Filled with self-righteousness (and enough nor-epinephrine to seriously jack up a small island civilization) she rushed up the remaining five flights of stairs. She inhaled deep as she passed through clouds of methane and mosquitoes, knowing she was close to her front door. As she approached the door she felt a series of sick, wracking spasms tear through her body with the heat of white phosphor. She retched onto her own feet and felt the fluid slide between her toes. Thick with protein and jellyfish nematocysts, the vomit stung her skin before the floor absorbed it.

"This is ridiculous!" she thought. "If they cut back my morphine ration one more time…" The thought was cut short by another string of dopesick gut explosions, all white fire and needles.

Eventually she composed herself and continued dragging the man in the diaper.

Once she and the patient were finally inside she closed the door of her secret apartment behind her. The slamming of the door woke James Toddle. His waking was brief. The moment he saw Nurse Sebac looking back at him with the waving stalks of her optic nerves he returned to his blessed unconsciousness.

The seeping purple lights that crawled across Nurse Sebac's ceiling were infested with wasps, the result of a failed "Nest-to-Chest" hive transplant she'd tried to perform weeks before. She'd even coated the patient's lungs with wasp pheromones, but once she set the hive free they instantly swarmed her overhead lighting and defiled it. Now her lighting had a strange buzz to it, worse than the old fluorescents in some of the surgical theaters. The constant, taunting sound of the buzz, amplified by her pain-killer withdrawals, crept into her head and haunted her.

Buzzbuzz you'll never be a Doctor *buzzbuzz* you've failed again *buzzbuzz* nice legs, tadpole *buzzbuzz* who are you fooling *buzzbuzz* dilantin is for Doctors *buzzbuzz* ha, only twelve surgeries in and you couldn't keep him alive *buzzbuzz* we're reducing your dosage levels *buzzbuzz* you'll just have to make due with less.

"Less" was eating her alive! She needed the *steady*, gratuitous supply of chemicals enjoyed by the Surgeons. And why not? She was just as creative as they were. She was the one that came up with Arterial Spraypainting. She was the one who fed hunger stimulants to patient's tapeworms. Pearls before surgical swine.

She had toyed with the idea that appearing Surgeon-like might earn her some kind of sedative stipend. She had amputated her legs and rigged up an elaborate pulley system, trying to feign leglessness in the surgical theater. They spotted the ruse instantly and spent the afternoon playing tetherball with her suspended torso. When they were done playing with her they even reattached her damn legs, which was *so* embarrassing.

No, the only way to get any real attention around here was through the rendering of the patients. She'd have to create a true abomination, something so abhorrent that everyone would expect nature to destroy it at any moment.

She had a chance to show her superiors what she was capable of. That chance was resting on the floor with his thumb in his mouth, dreaming of something and nursing furiously hard. He was her grand and horrible infant, the perfect patient for her plan.

"Well," she thought "I better get to gettin' on with it."

She ground her jaw in determination, spit out a shattered tooth, and swung her leg forward as fast as she could into the soft midsection of James Toddle, patient-at-large.

"Borf!" he exclaimed, followed by, "Ooooooooohhhhhhh!"

Then he began to cry, all red-faced wailing and high decibel screeching.

He didn't stop crying until she force-fed him a tube of high-powered verdalax, known for its ability to trigger violent, gushing outbursts of truth (after, of course, the horrible onset of gut cramping). She waited a few minutes for the medicine to invade. Then she asked one question and watched the floodgates open.

"James, how did you get here?"

Glassy-eyed and hypnotized, James Toddle let it all out in a great cathartic babble, a torrent of nonsense that left impact ripples in Nurse Sebac's car puddles.

"I just, well, I like wearing diapers, and one of my Momma's, one of them that I paid for, back when I was a popular baby, she paid for the electrolysis so I could be officially baby-like, and you can get awful poor buying these oversized diapers, and I just like to nurse and they wouldn't let me wear my bonnet to work so I was all done for and the rubber pants were what I wanted and my little brother was born and they took away *my* diapers and gave them to *him*, and paid attention to *him*, and they didn't care about *me* anymore, 'cause I wasn't in the diapers, so then I paid *real close* attention to my little brother until his head was black and then I ran away and I was all alone again and then I met one of my new Mommas and she took me in and I fell in love with her and one night she wouldn't feed me so *I had to* eat some of her soft parts and then I got sent to a special hospital and they said I had an Edible Oedipal complex that was *really* complex, but at least at the hospital they let me wear my diapers as long as I kept making dirties in them, and then one day I woke up and the hospital wall was missing like it blew up, and the bricks were smoking, and a man with a metal cage over his mouth asked me if I wanted to go to a better hospital and then he stuck a pokey in me and I woke up here and now I'm with you and I hope you're my new Momster, 'cause I'm hungry, so hungry…"

James Toddle was drooling.

Nurse Sebac opened her arms and freed one sagging grey breast from her filthy scrubs. She leaned over James and put it in his mouth and squeezed it with one hand until thick black oil that smelled like curdled milk sprayed into his throat. James lapped it up for his new Momster, basking in the udder attention until his throat grew numb and his brain was carpeted, and gravity lost its hold on everything.

The procedure went perfectly. Between periodic feedings of Nurse Sebac's obsidian dark and highly anesthetic milk, James Toddle was shrinking. She was giving him super-doses of atropherone, a regressive growth hormone originally used to shrink cows to "Kickin' Size." After six successful super-dosings, James was just the right size to fit in her new machine. Smaller than a bread basket, bigger than the average human brain.

Even with an ocean of anesthetic in his system, James Toddle looked uncomfortable shrinking to his desired baby size. He began to scream when the plates in his skull de-fused and separated, but a mottled grey teat ended his tantrum.

Nurse Sebac made sure he was awake when she pulled back the tarps in the corner of her room to reveal the machine she had built but never had a chance to test.

James Toddle's eyes flashed wide in their milky haze as he saw the unveiling.

"I call it The Woom, James. You, my lovely child, are the first to take it for a test drive."

It floated three feet above the floor, a grotesque amalgam of human skin, horse hide, solidified secretions, mortar, brick, viscera, and plastic tubing.

The Woom began to quiver as Nurse Sebac brought James Toddle closer to it.

She pinched his right cheek and said, "See you in nine minutes."

Nurse Sebac lifted a fleshy fold at the base of the machine and pushed James into The Woom.

A mucus plug coagulated into place beneath James Toddle and he felt the walls around him grow closer. Fluid rushed in and he found he could breathe the green and black ichors into his lungs. The fluid was filled with luminescent brine that labored away at creating the new James. He floated there, tiny, in the machine that was numbing him and re-shaping him, and thought, "Finally, back where I belong."

Nine minutes later, he was re-born. A fissure opened in the base of the machine and belched him out with a few gallons of amniotic fluid. His eyes were fused together and his nose emerged from his forehead like an inverted sink spigot. His mouth was fish-thin, and he could barely breathe.

Nurse Sebac took one look at him and said, "Now, that simply won't do. You won't survive long enough for me to show the boys downstairs. I better run you through the seed cleaner."

She opened a metal door at the top of The Woom and placed him inside again. Ropes of intestine slid around him, squeezing the breath from him. Cone spiders scuttled around him and sucked away his vital fluids. The brick walls on each side of him throbbed with the heat of a blast furnace and dried him until he was just a husk. He felt one of the spiders bore into the side of his head and pull *him* out of his skull, and he felt his consciousness being carried along and dropped down a long tube, back into the warmth and darkness at the base of The Woom. His consciousness, the germ of him, planted its seed and he grew. As he gestated he pictured himself as the perfect man, with a newscaster's hair and a car dealer's smile, someone so normal that all Moms would have to love him, and care for him forever. He tried to grow *just right*. Nine minutes later he was back in his new Momster's arms.

"Oh, James! The four external livers are fine, but that adorable blonde hair has got to go! Try harder this time; I want something really good to show for my hard work. I've got to show those uppity floating fucks something spectacular or I'll never be able to advance!"

James felt Nurse Sebac's hands shaking as she picked him up.

No matter how many times James Toddle was born, he wouldn't come out just right. Sure, he'd have a vestigal wing here, a monstrous case of hydropedalism there, but parts of him remained cherubic in contrast. It was never enough for Nurse Sebac, who credited herself as a bit of a perfectionist. The remaining will of James Toddle, the part of him that really wanted a Mom to love him, counteracted the designs of The Woom just enough to subvert its intentions. He wanted a Momster, Nurse Sebac wanted a monster.

He was born with a scaly foot sticking out of his abdomen and a button nose. He was born with rosy cheeks and assholes for eyes.

James felt hungrier and more alone with each birth. When he had limbs he would reach for his new Mom and try to cling to her. On the forty-eighth birth he managed to wind a white and jellied tentacle around her waist, but she clipped it off with a rib saw and forced him back into the seed cleaner. On the ninety-fourth birth he burrowed halfway into her thigh with his new circular mouth, but she poured salt on him and he shriveled.

After the hundredth birth James gave up hope and was sick of being born again. He had no options. No matter how he felt, he was still born.

Hope left him. Despair filled The Woom and his incarnations became more and more horrible. His one hundred and forty-fifth birth went perfectly.

At last! He saw her eyes flash with adoration and a mother's love.

"Oh my! Toothy phalluses, inverted eyes, an antler shaped skull, and cleft palate! I'm the luckiest mother in the world! I can't wait to show you off!"

He could see her infected injection points were salivating, anticipating oxycontin appetizers.

He watched her recognize the mirrored hunger and need in his new, jet-black eyes.

She picked him up to feed.

James Toddle fed for two days, then abandoned her corpse. After he ate her heart he was positive that she had no more love to give. He had swallowed the source.

He blamed the cold Mother-husk on the floor for his newfound loneliness. If she really loved him she'd keep on giving. All he needed was to be fed, and loved, and cherished.

His new Mom had grown cold to him after time, like the others before her. This Mom had grown cold *and* stiff, so once again he was on his own. He would need to find another Mother, one who would recognize him for the tiny miracle he was and never stop the flow of food and love that he required. He'd just have to try harder. He'd have to be the perfect child.

He shambled along the halls of the Facility in search of a new Mom. He tried, in spite of the prolapsed colon hanging wet from his neck and the stinking fluid ejaculated from the pulsing flesh protruding from his mouth, to feel wondrous and sweet and treasured.

Love, after all, was his birthright.

PRECEDENTS

The smell of toilet-brewed sterno fills Cell 5-11 of the LaGrange Penitentiary. Marcia Grable is watching her cell-mate, abusive baby-sitter Tracy Everton, take toxic slugs of the shit-tinged prison moonshine.

Marcia is not at all surprised when Tracy passes out and hits the concrete floor with a wet, fleshy smack. Marcia is surprised to find herself laughing, and hard, to the point where her chest aches from it and she feels half crazy. Something about that sound, the loose body slapping the ground, echoes deep inside of her.

It reminds her of the sound of Josh Grable's last moment on Earth.

Back up.

Marcia presses her forehead against the cold window of the prison transit bus and watches the wheat fields roll by until they become a beige blur. She tries to contain the anger that burns holes in her stomach. The handcuffs, secured tight to the seat railing, twist against her wrists and rub her skin red and raw till it throbs.

She remembers the courtroom photograph of Josh's corpse, his lips blue as Arctic glaciers, his hair much lighter than it had been the day before his death.

She tries to feel remorse. She knows it's part of her sentence, but the feeling never comes.

"If they only knew him, if they saw the way he looked at me, with those eyes... nothing but shark eyes. Just empty. If they knew, I'd be a free woman. If they knew..."

She thinks like this for hours, as her stomach eats itself and bile rises in her throat.

"If they knew my husband like I did, they'd have done the same."

Back up.

The jury foreman reads the sentence so calm you'd think he was reading lawnmower assembly instructions.

Then the monotone voice of the jury foreman drops the word "Guilty" and it hits Marcia's heart sledgehammer heavy.

A black veil pulls itself over her eyes...

She wakes seconds later, her whole body tingling as she regains consciousness, hearing her good-for-nothing state appointed lawyer yelling.

"Give her some room, she needs air."

Guilty.

"Fuck air," she thinks, "I need a new lawyer." There is no humor in the thought, only despair on the verge of resignation.

Two days later she steps onto the prison bus and winces as they tighten her handcuffs to the seat railing.

Back up.

Marcia's lawyer is going over the details, the ugly details, during her deposition. He says the state has a very strong case, and they've already secured the librarian and the store clerk to testify. He says the doorknob is an incredibly damaging piece of evidence. The jury will have to know everything, every nasty little detail of her private life, in order to build sympathy for her case.

It's going to be rough, he says. The defense will play up Josh's childhood, with its daily abuses and lingering scars. They'll try to shift the blame back a generation, to Josh's father, Darren. They'll make Marcia the monster and turn Josh into a sympathetically scarred psyche incapable of escaping his childhood hell.

"And the jurors will eat it up, Marcia. This is a jury of your peers. They watch the same TV movies. They belong to Oprah's Book Club. You can take any monster, slap a bad dad into his past, and all of a sudden he's just another lost soul, lashing out. And you were the poor lady that got in the way. They'll argue *you* lacked compassion. You were the one that took things too far."

The defense's plan makes sense to her. She can't even count the number of nights she'd spent trying to blame her own mother for telling her, "Marriage demands compromise." Shifting the blame is so easy. The cheapest freedom she'd ever found. But nothing can justify what Josh did...

"They can't do that. I never even met his father. Everything Josh did, he did of his own free will."

"You talk like that, Marcia, you put that point of view into *your* testimony and you'll kill our case. If we can't blame Josh for what *you* did..."

And her crime, he says, comes across as too calculated.

"I wish you could have committed a simple crime of passion. People who commit crimes of passion often get off with manslaughter. People can sympathize with lover's rage. People can put themselves in that position, they can feel their own finger on the trigger, anxious to squeeze."

Marcia says nothing.

"What you did, Marcia, will not be construed as a crime of passion. Your actions involved too much forethought. We'll be lucky to get a life sentence. You have chosen to commit what will be perceived as a coldhearted murder in a state very fond of capital punishment."

Marcia is staring at the tile floor, agonizing at the thought of airing her family's dirty laundry. Her mind flashes on a syringe full of strychnine, a thumb hovering over the plunger.

"So, where do I begin?"

Back up.

Marcia is at her friend Theresa's house when the police cruiser pulls up.

Her first thought creates a sick panic in her heart.

"I haven't finished cleaning up yet...maybe they're just here to ask questions... whereabouts...something...oh God...if they've been to the house...oh shit...I haven't fixed the doorknob yet. That fucking doorknob...this is too soon. I was supposed to make the call. So who called? His boss? Was he supposed to work today? Oh, God. Oh, God, he was. Shit, okay, play it straight, ride this out. You were cleaning the house, then you spent the night here. That's it. God, please..."

She has been preparing for this moment, and when the cop breaks the news about Josh's death she shakes and her hands tremble, and the tears well up, and she mutters, "This just can't be."

She had read on the internet that denial was supposed to be her first response.

"This just can't be, officer."

She hopes her nervousness reads as shock. She fights back an incredibly strange urge to smile.

The urge to smile disappears as the handcuffs cut into her wrists.

Back up.

Marcia drives to her friend Theresa's house at four in the morning. She is fighting back an urge to laugh, afraid the sound of her own voice would resonate as distant, crazy. She has her windows rolled down, hoping to cleanse herself of the smell. She drives just two miles over the speed limit, knowing that getting pulled over right now would destroy her alibi.

"I'll get to Theresa's and we'll have a cup of tea and we'll watch the sun rise. How long has it been since I've seen the sunrise?"

Too damn long, she concludes, and she laughs, and it does make her feel crazy, but it feels better than being afraid.

Back up.

Marcia opens every window in every room of her small manufactured home. She grabs her keys off the kitchen counter, puts them in her pocket, and then heads back to the bathroom. She picks up the towel pressed tight against the bottom of the door and shuffles away, careful not to inhale deeply until she reaches the kitchen. She grabs a plastic container from beneath the kitchen sink, and carries it, along with the towel, to her backyard, where she has ignited a burn barrel. She drops the items in and watches as they both glow green. Her eyes follow the thick black plumes of swirling smoke as they rise towards the stars.

Back up.

Josh Grable suddenly sounds very sober as he yells, "Marcia, help me out here, let me out of this fucking bathroom or I swear to God..."

His screams are interrupted by violent, retching coughs, and he pounds on the door with enough force that she hears the wood splintering, and just for one second she thinks he may live, and oh God if he gets out of there he's going to torture me, he's going to tear me to pieces, he's going to kill me.

"Please, God," she thinks.

Her prayer is answered by the sound of his body hitting the ground with a wet, fleshy smack as the toilet flushes behind him.

She is confronted by an unexpected surge of tears, sitting cross-legged on the floor, waiting for him to die. Her tears dry quickly as she remembers why this must happen.

She waits for a few minutes to confirm his death, through his silence. Once she feels confident of the fact she cleans up, pulling the duct tape off of the outside of the bathroom window, opening the windows in every room of the house.

"My husband's had a horrible accident," she thinks.

"Thank God."

Back up.

Marcia lies in the dark, feeling Josh's sweat cool on her body. "He drank two bottles. He'll have to piss sooner or later."

She waits, her heart beating hummingbird fast in the dark room, hoping he won't pass out.

After twenty minutes he finally rises from the bed and staggers to the bathroom. She pads softly behind him, and when he closes the door she locks it as quietly as she can from the outside, and grabs the towel she'd placed in the nearby closet. She pushes the towel as tight as she can between the carpet and the door, knowing her life depends on covering that gap.

She hears his urine splattering against the porcelain, a few spurts and then a long steady stream. She hears him gasp for air, and then he makes a loud gagging noise. She sees the doorknob jiggle, then shake violently. It takes Josh a long, drunken moment to realize the doorknob's been locked from the outside.

Marcia hears his voice, confused, desperate.

"Marsh, wake up! Help me out here!"

"I'm right here, Josh."

"Marsh, I think I'm in trouble here! I can barely breathe! My fuckin' eyes... oh shit... aaah... Marsh, open the door, it's broke or somethin'!"

"No."

"Oh shit, honey, I can't...ah...I...what the fuck is going on here? Open the Goddamned door!"

Silence.

"Marsh... this isn't funny... you're gonna... I mean, is this about the other night... I'm sorry, Marsh, I'm real sorry about all that... now quit playing your little games and OPEN THE FUCKING DOOR!"

"Fuck you."

"Marcia, help me out here..."

Back up.

Marcia's day speeds by, and an almost giddy feeling fills her body as she does her shopping. At a Shop Rite she purchases a new lock for the bathroom door; a few air fresheners for her car, the little tree shaped ones, three bottles of Sheppard Springs merlot, and a box of Wheat Snacks.

She drives across town to the Home Value wholesalers and makes a few inquiries with a store clerk about cleaning products. She asks about their respective strengths, how concentrated they are, and which ones are really industrial potency. The look on the face of the store clerk says he's never seen anyone so excited about cleaning products in his entire life.

Then Marcia drives home and works frantically, breaking out

in cold sweats and hot flashes as she prepares for Josh to come home. She puts a gouge into her left thumb as she replaces the bathroom lock with the new one she purchased. It is the exact same model, but once she finishes installing it, the lock is on the outside.

She then heads into the bathroom and carefully bails out the toilet water currently sitting in the bowl. Cup by cup, she pours it down the sink. She uncaps her Home Value purchase and empties its contents into the bowl. The smell is so strong she recoils. It feels like a butane torch burning inside of her lungs, so she exits quickly and leaves the door just a tiny crack open.

By the time Josh gets home and takes off his Berwood Mall Security outfit she's already got a bottle of red wine cracked and she nearly pours it down his throat and kisses his neck and tells him she wants it to be like old times, she wants to party and so they party and skip dinner and she drinks one bottle and he sucks down the two others and then he pulls her into the bedroom and he's rubbing his crotch and mumbling to himself and she's nervous cause he's looking at her with those empty shark eyes and she doesn't want to get hurt so she goes to him and he smashes himself into her and pushes down on top of her but he's so drunk he can't get it in and he tries and he wraps his arms around her and squeezes hard, too hard and she can't breathe, and she starts to panic and he looks in her eyes like he wants to just crush her away into nothing and sweat drips from his forehead onto her face and he suddenly gives and rolls off of her and they lie there.

Marcia hates him more than ever.

Eventually he rises and stumbles to the bathroom.

Back up.

The librarian was very helpful, and showed Marcia how to use the internet properly, how to hold the mouse and enter keywords like "grieving process."

The computer, intended for public use, records every page Marcia visits.

The page that talks about safety and cleaning products.

The page that teaches her the cogeners in red wines and dark alcoholic beverages increases the level of ammonia in urine.

The page about dealing with the loss of a loved one.

Marcia makes an impression.

Back up.

Theresa opens the door to her house and finds Marcia sobbing on her stoop.

Minutes later, after Marcia tells her story, Theresa makes a suggestion. Theresa says, "A man like that deserves to fucking die. I see this sort of thing on TV all the time. Drunken husband, abused wife. A lot of these wives, even if they leave, they're the ones that end up dead."

She then proceeds to make other suggestions, talking up counseling and police intervention. It doesn't matter, because inside Marcia's head she hears Theresa saying, over and over again, "A man like that deserves to fucking die." These words echo deep. They set into her bones, take hold behind her eyes.

Theresa makes an impression.

Back up.

Marcia sits on the toilet, weeping, holding her bruised back and her belly.

The water in the toilet beneath her is dark crimson.

Her mind is sick with pain, trembling in her head as she thinks, "Oh, God, please let me have him back, please let me have Hollis back, I swear I'm sorry for whatever I've done that made this happen, I swear, God please let me have him back, he wasn't even born and I would have loved him so good, and he would have loved me back, and loved me, nobody loves me, please God..."

She sits there for two hours as the water beneath her grows darker and her skin grows cold.

Back up.

She is asleep and doesn't want to wake up. Josh comes home late and rotten with booze. He tries to crawl on top of her and she pushes him back.

His eyes change.

He changes. He leaves his heart in the space behind him and

moves forward like a machine. He makes fists, his knuckles crack.

She curls up in a ball and lets him hit her until he collapses, like he always does.

He grunts and hisses out breath hot with alcohol as his hands crunch into her body.

He doesn't know she's six weeks late for her period.

He falls asleep with his knuckles purple, and doesn't wake as Marcia crawls to the bathroom.

Back up. Back up. Back up.

Marcia is fifteen, and pays very close attention to her Home Ec. teacher when he emphasizes the danger of mixing ammonia and bleach when cleaning your house.

"They call it chlorine gas, people, and it killed thousands in World War I. Don't let it kill you because you're not paying attention."

The lesson makes an impression.

Back up.

Marcia is five and asks her Mom what she dreamed of being when she grew up. Her mom says, "I just wanted to have a beautiful baby and a kind husband to take care of and love. That's all I ever wanted, really."

Marcia agrees that it's about the loveliest dream she's ever heard of.

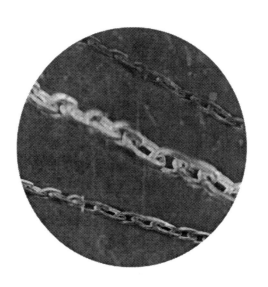

STANLEY'S LIPS

I first noticed his lips when I was watching late night televison.

I was curled up in my favorite patchwork blanket with a pillow firmly planted between my lower back and the armrest of my couch. I was nodding off to Friday Night Videos when one particular thing caught my attention. The lips of rock "artist" Stanley Kremer, lead singer for The Bushmen, a free form jazz group.

In the video Stanley was wearing a serape and playing bongos. In order to convince the audience that he was feeling the groove of his bongo solo he was swinging his hunched shoulders back and forth and contorting his face. His face was constantly shifting into the sort of rictus that normally only accompanies a well filmed "money shot." His lips pulled back so far at some point that every single one of his teeth were visible. It was hideous. His upper lip actually seemed stuck in the groove above his gums, and the video cut away, but if the camera would have remained on him I'm fairly sure I would have witnessed a couple of P.A.'s using warm water and rubber tipped pliers to shift his lips back into place.

Now, when someone begins to smile or grimace or simply speak I see Stanley for a brief second, in the shifting of their lips, the spreading of the vermillion border. And I want to reach out and grab the person's lips and restrain them from receding any further.

I don't tell jokes anymore. Chickens with dicks in them have ceased their road crossing. When I tell jokes, people smile. And when they smile they do so with Stanley's lips, his sick death's-head grin. Every toothy face is his now. My mind is re-making humanity's face, Stanley-style.

Julia Roberts- well, I about piss my pants if I see her.

A dream two nights ago: I am speaking in front of a crowd at a massive red tinted auditorium. I am telling them something about deep core drilling and the benefits thereof. They are nodding and listening quietly and intently. For a clever finisher I tell a joke about three dwarves whistling while they worked. The crowd smiles.

Then Stanley steps into the center of the auditorium. He is applauding, and then, like an old west gunslinger, he swiftly pulls his bongos out from behind his back, attached to a rope around his neck, and begins to pound at them. He shouts out to the audience and I, yelling that in Africa the best drummers have blood in their urine because of all the broken capillaries in their hands. The blood has to work its way out. He holds up his own hands, and the bongos are still ringing out like boo-doo-doo-boo-do. His hands are throbbing red, and the skin of his palms is pulled tight to bursting from all the blood that bloats them. He begins to play again and his palms explode as they hit the drums. Flecks of blood spray from his raw hands onto the audience. The entire auditorium is filled with people swaying zombie-like to Stanley's bongos and as his beats reach a white hot pitch they all begin to smile, and all of them have Stanley's lips, pulled tight to their skulls like two strips of dried liver. Then, they stand and applaud. I take a bow and they all begin to move to the stage, drool slipping from the edges of their mouths.

The next day I looked in my copy of Freud's Dreams and Analysis and learned that my nightmare meant I'm afraid of vaginas and dogs. "Freud was a coke-head asshole," I joke to myself. But I don't smile. There are mirrors nearby, with Stanley hiding beneath the surface.

SNOWFALL

Despite Jake's profound deafness, he swore for a moment that he'd heard something. He'd at least felt the sound, a tremble in his small, feather-light bones. This pushing noise that seemed for a moment to sit on his chest and trap his breath in his lungs, it brought him from deep sleep to a sort of half-awake that didn't feel real.

He stayed in this space between dream and waking for awhile, barely shaking in his hammock bed which was buoyed by a loose spring at each end. Deaf since age three, Jake had developed a "feel" for sound, and thought it best to ignore the immense noise that had tried to shake him from his warm slumber. The sound was too big, a sound for Mom and Dad to investigate and deal with.

There was a moment following the noise when the temperature in his basement room soared, and Jake shifted from side to side, sweltering in the heat and memories of the fever that had stolen sound from his young body. He stirred and gently cried, the tears rolling almost cool over his burning cheeks.

He woke three hours later, in a pitch black room full of stale air. He was sweating in his pajamas, and his lower back felt clammy, slick. He tossed aside the down comforter his parents bought him last year for his fifth birthday, eager to feel some cool air on his sticky skin. He swung his legs over the side of the hammock and dismounted with a small hop. His feet slapped the floor of the basement. Cold sank into the pads of his toes and his heels. He wished his whole body could be filled with that cold, and thought for a half-second about taking off his grey pajamas and lying naked on the floor. His stomach, grumbling and contracting tight, suggested another agenda.

Jake rubbed the sleep out of his eyes and flicked it off of his fingers. It took him twelve shuffling steps in the dark to find the far left wall where the staircase was. It was his staircase, the entrance to his lair, his room, his favorite place in the whole house. The wooden steps rising up to the kitchen entrance were trampled smooth by his constant trespass. Halfway up the stairs he knew he would find the light switch.

Jake stepped with care up to the middle of the staircase. His small hand reached through the dark and silence of the basement and he found comfort as he touched rigid plastic. He flipped the switch up, expecting to see the soft light of the bare bulb hanging central to the room. Instead he saw continued darkness, pervasive. He flipped the switch up and down, up and down, with the same result. This happened once before, and he had told Dad, and Dad had run down to the basement with a flashlight and put a fresh bulb in the socket while Jake sat upstairs slurping sugary cereal milk from the bottom of his favorite bowl, the one with the red fishes on it.

The thought of cereal re-oriented Jake, and he padded up to the top of the stairs. He thought that he'd tell Dad about the light bulb later, and Dad would fix it because that's all the light Jake got down there. Jake chose to live in the basement, even though it had no windows. To Jake it felt like a hideout, a secret dungeon, and it saved him from sharing a room with his two older brothers, Doug and Sean.

Jake opened the door and stepped into the kitchen, which was also dark, although not jet black like his room. The kitchen was awash in the soft grey light that slipped in through the cracks of the curtains.

He walked over to the light switch by the stove and flipped it. No result. He stood in the dim grey light, confused. He thought every light bulb in the house must have broken on the same day.

He opened the fridge and a soft wave of cool air embraced him, causing goosebumps. He couldn't believe what he saw inside. The fridge light was out too. It didn't matter; he knew exactly where Mom kept the chocolate milk. He opened the flaps, and even though he knew it was trouble, started drinking right from the carton. He gulped back the thick chocolate milk with his lips pressed tight against the waxed cardboard, to keep from getting a brown moustache. He closed the carton and stuck it back in the fridge.

With the sweet milk resting in his belly he became more curious than hungry, and wondered where his parents were. Either Mom or Dad usually waited around with him until Marcy showed up.

Jake loved Marcy, the lady that took care of him during the summer while his parents and brothers worked. She smelled like cucumbers and brown sugar, and Mom said she was the only nanny in the county who knew sign language. She also knew where Mom hid the Tootsie Rolls, and when Jake figured something out Marcy would give him a handful. Jake only ate a couple of them a day, relishing the thick texture and the way they filled his senses as he chewed. The surplus Tootsie Rolls he saved were stashed in a brown paper bag that he hid at the bottom of his toy chest.

Jake noticed that the house felt smaller in the dark. Mom said that the house was little and cheap since the Army used to keep soldiers in it. She said that when the base moved to the other side of town the old concrete soldier houses got fixed up and sold off. This made Jake feel safe, like he lived in a castle made for warriors. He thought maybe someday he'd be a soldier.

He began to feel strange as he crept through the house, looking for someone, anyone. He wished, as he often did, that he could hear. He would just tune his ears in and follow the sound of his Mom or his Dad to the source, like he used to before he got sick and hot and the world became silent.

Every room in the house was empty, and Jake began to worry, and figured that Marcy must be on her way. Otherwise his parents never would have left him alone.

He walked into the living room and sat down in front of the

television. He thought he'd watch some cartoons and before he knew it Marcy would be at the door, smelling like sugar.

The T.V. wouldn't work either, which was probably for the best. Mom and Dad didn't let him watch any shows for the last couple of weeks. They said there was nothing but the news on anyway, and he got scared when he watched the news.

Anxious, and a little worried, Jake crawled over to the window at the front of the house. He reached up and pressed his hand to the heavy, dark green velvet drapes. He pushed them to the left, looked outside, and understood what was going on.

It was snowing, and in the middle of Summer no less! The electricity must not work when it gets cold in the Summer. Mom and Dad were probably outside, shoveling the driveway or the roof.

Jake placed his right palm, open, against the glass of the window to see how cold it was. The glass was warm, almost hot, and Jake noticed his breath wasn't freezing on it.

The idea of a Summer snowstorm filled Jake with a sense of wonder and excitement. He thought for a second that maybe God was giving him this miracle to apologize for making him deaf, but he felt instantly guilty for thinking so.

Jake stood up and walked to the front door. His hand reached to the doorknob and found it was warm. Overjoyed at the thought of this unexpected Winter he threw the front door open and ran outside.

The snow was virgin, and rested a foot thick across the whole neighborhood. Clouds hung heavy and black across the sky, and Jake saw flashes of lightning trapped within them. He looked for the sun in every direction and saw only clouds, and the peculiar grey light that matched his pajamas. He wasn't cold, and felt the shift of a warm breeze across his skin.

Jake didn't see a single person outside, including his parents, but the miracle of Summertime Winter had filled his mind to bursting, and he didn't worry. He was amazed by the storm. The grey snowflakes were coming down so thick he couldn't see across the street.

He held out his hands and caught some of the flakes in his palms. They would not melt, and when he blew his hot breath on them they didn't turn to water. Instead they fell to pieces and swirled away.

He trudged out to the center of his front yard and turned around, gazing at his house in the dusky light.

He couldn't believe his eyes. Someone had painted his whole house the darkest black he'd ever seen. On top of that, they'd painted people, beautiful, bright white people, on the front of his house. There were two people running, maybe playing, and standing closer to the door, near the front windows, the silhouettes of his parents stood with arms outstretched to the sky.

Jake was laughing as he looked at the mural, a soft, rasping laugh that felt good in his throat. Wouldn't Marcy be surprised when she saw the painting?

Upon seeing the shapes of his parents Jake was filled with a sense of their absence, and couldn't wait to see them after work. For now, he could play.

He lay down on his back in the warm sheet of snow that blanketed his front yard and began to move his legs and arms slowly, rhythmically, up and down.

As he packed the soft ground beneath him he felt the wind change directions, blowing fast and warm against the left side of his face.

Jake perfected his snow angel and took a moment to appreciate what he had created. He inhaled deeply, instilled with a sense of calm as his chest rose.

Jake watched the snow drift down, blinking and laughing as it landed on his eyelashes.

He let the hot wind flow over him. It soon filled the air with color, and Jake inhaled its lullaby deep into his body.

He slept quiet in the arms of his angel, while the misplaced Winter stormed around him.

EX-HALE

I see a lot of familiar faces out there in the audience tonight. Friends, family, co-workers, loved ones. I'm sure that Ray would be glad you all showed up. Ray really appreciated all of you. Well, except for Mark Clemont. Mark, what are you doing here? Get out!... We're all waiting, Mark.... Mark, just show some decency and go... Mark, Jesus Christ, no you can't see the body... no, you know it's closed casket only... Mark, do us all a favor and go before we have to call security... are you drunk, Mark?...look man, now Ray's mom is crying... yeah, well I guess we can't pin that one on you, but you sure aren't helping things... no, I don't want to take this outside...always the macho man, Mark, big tough Mark, Mr. Tough Guy, you're so sad, man...Oh, I'm the sad one, well you're sadder...hey, fuck you!...what does my wife have to do with this...Jesus Christ, Mark, you are such a liar...look what you made me do, I just blasphemed in a church...I don't care if you don't believe in God, Mark, that has nothing to do with any of this... well I'm sure you'll believe when you are burning in hell...say one more word, Mark, one more motherfucking word, and I swear to you the cemetery will clear a spot for you, right next to Ray...yes, yes, you're right, Mark, we're the stupid ones, and you are Mr. Smart...bye, Mark!

OK, now that we got that over with, let's remember Ray.

Ray was a Morgy. For those of you out there who aren't familiar with the jargon of Ray's industry, that means he played corpses in the motion pictures. Ray did over 40 films in his day. He was amazing, I mean any of the other Morgy's would tell you that. When it came to remaining inanimate for a long period of time Ray was like a praying mantis. Beautiful, man, beautiful. Unfortunately, like all of us who work too much, he started to make little flubs. You could see him breathing. The breathing corpse in The Devil's Own, that was Ray. He had started to blink too, which is never good. Ray was such an overachiever, he just wanted to entertain, and when he started slipping, he took drastic measures. After he was fired from the set of Ilsa's Seduction 3 for breathing, he had his lungs medically removed. The authorities are still looking for the doctor. Ray did not survive long without his lungs. Actually three days was much longer than anyone expected him to live, so there's even more proof of what an amazing guy he was.

The thing is, I think maybe Ray wanted it this way. I mean, this is his ultimate performance right here.

Immaculate. Perfect.

He has certainly convinced all of us that he is dead.

Congratulations, Ray! You're the best, man.

The best.

WORKING AT HOME

A needle sharp moment of pain in Dr. Frank Challing's ankle distracts him for less than a second, and is easily brushed off. His brain is otherwise occupied, a maelstrom of activity as he learns that his memories of the day's events won't wipe clean, no matter how hard he tries to ignore or deny them. He attempts to keep his brain free of thought through labor. He sweeps, mops, scrubs, polishes, and drips salt sweat from his slick forehead as he compulsively brings the entire kitchen to a smooth luster.

His hard work fails in the face of his memory, and every time his eyelids close together he can see the nightmare in full color.

The girl is there, torn to tatters.

The strange doctors are there, holding him, watching her, waiting for the things to finish eating.

Mr. Devries had told him, "You mustn't think too deeply about it, Frank."

Mr. Devries hadn't been present at the phlebotomy lab today, and had no idea how impossible executing his recommendation would be. Mr. Devries didn't have to throw his clothes in the incinerator today. Mr. Devries did not spend three hours in quarantine. Mr. Devries had not had to watch *them*.

Dr. Frank Challing is suddenly racked with shudders and a greasy cold sweat.

He looks in desperation around the kitchen and finds it in immaculate status, clean enough to satisfy a legion of anal-retentive Martha Stewart acolytes. It takes him three seconds to get to the liquor cabinet. It is the first time he has ever felt like he lunged for something, and it shocks him. He grabs a bottle of Hennessey but does not bother to look through the cabinet for his favorite snifter, the one he got in his High Roller's Suite at Luxor.

A rapid twist of his left thumb leaves the cap of the bottle plunging to the floor, making a plastic click as it strikes the ground. The first slug goes back like water, as does the second, and it's only on the fifth gulp that he feels flush, his skin tingling. Frank Challing almost makes a tight face in reaction to the gasoline burn in his belly and throat, but restrains himself. He has always seen the post-liquor cringe as a sign of weakness and lack of personal control.

You and your control, Frank! Just live for once.

He hasn't heard the real thing in three years, but his ex-wife's voice still gets on his nerves from time to time.

Oh, so you won't talk to me about your work, huh? You sure don't mind talking to that bottle.

"She was always so damned dramatic," Frank thinks as he walks into his entertainment room and sets the bottle of cognac on the coffee table in front of him. He hangs his head and sighs. The sigh is stertorous and thick, and to Frank's discomfort, more than a little shaky. "Jesus, calm down, Frank!" he demands, addressing himself in the empty room. He can hear the slight electric hum of his refrigerator in the kitchen, and it makes him uneasy.

It is quiet enough for him to think.

I don't even know what her name was. She never said anything. All she could do was scream while those things...

Frank Challing's thoughts are interrupted by a sound he does not recognize. He picks up his bottle of cognac and walks towards the sound coming from the bay windows on the far west side of his loft.

"Is someone humming in here?" he wonders. His feet tread softly across the cold floor as he approaches his windows. As he nears the edge of his loft a gust of wind speeds across the black tinted surface of the bay windows, howling first, then reducing to a high pitched whisper.

"The wind must be blowing sixty miles an hour out there. It's making my damn windows vibrate," he thinks. "Could the pressure suck my windows out of the building?"

He pictures himself sucked out with the windows, twisting like a leaf in the screaming winds until he and the glass panels hit the pavement at the same time. Rough cleanup. He shivers again.

Frank takes his ninth and tenth gulps off the bottle, which has grown significantly lighter. This sensation of decreased weight barely registers in his mind. Frank also pays little notice to the slight itch on his inner right ankle turning into a burning sensation. Frank is too buzzed to notice the small but spreading red spot on the side of his white Avia sock.

He sees a blinking red light in the corner of his left eye, and feels for a moment that he may pass out. He grabs onto a decorative Japanese hutch and steadies himself, lets the blood flow back into his head. "Thought I was about to go down. Better slow up on this shit." He sets the bottle down hard on the hutch.

As he revolves his head his sight takes a moment to catch up with the movement and then whips into position, arriving in his eyes with a liquid slosh, the effect of which is nauseating. He still sees the blinking red light out of his peripheral, and then realizes it's his answering machine. Blink, blink, pause... he has two messages.

His finger presses in the dust free plastic button marked "Play" and there are a few seconds of analog sounding hiss. At first he does not recognize the voice, and thinks it might be one of those damn telemarketers. Then, with a degree of shame, he realizes it is his daughter's voice.

"Hello...well, I hope I'm leaving this message in the right place 'cause there was no greeting or anything, your machine just beeps. Anyway, this message is for Frank Challing, and if I've got the right machine, then Hi, Dad! First of all I have to say I missed you at the wedding, and I totally disagree with Mom's politics on this... she's just... well, you know Mom. Enough of that, I just wanted to say thank you for the gift, Mark and I had a fabulous time in Nagano, and the skiing was absolutely gorgeous. So... thank you. Mom wouldn't give me your new phone number, she's burning bridges left and right, so I found you on the internet. This call cost me twenty bucks! Kidding! I just had to call, I miss you and I had this dream... I don't know... I just... never mind, now I feel kind of stupid. Anyway, again, thank you, and I miss you and love you! I can't wait to see you again, Daddy! You owe me a hug. My number and my address are still the same. Call me."

Frank, with one hand against the wall for balance, says, "I love you too, honey..." He feels grateful for her call. As another torrent of wind shakes the windows to his right he thinks, "Hell, I'm overjoyed if the phone company calls these days." Before Frank can feel a moment of the self-pity that he loathes and sees approaching, the second message starts.

"Francis, it's Devries. You must get a message on that machine of yours. I apologize for calling this time of the evening, but I must clarify a few things about today's incident for you. Listen very carefully; this is a matter of utmost security. Top brass at the hospital have decided to let you know certain things about both the patient and the illness that afflicted her. We will be sending an escort to your residence at seven tomorrow morning. You will accompany him to the hospital and receive full disclosure of the facts in this case. In the meantime, I must demand that you do not speak to anyone in regards to this matter, even your family. To do so could mean the endangerment of both your position at our facility and the security of the facility itself. You may be aware of the financial backing we've been receiving from a third party in certain areas of research. I don't feel anything else needs to be said. I will see you in the morning, Frank. Have a pleasant evening, and enjoy the storm. It should be quite dramatic."

Frank finds the whole message incredulous, and anger grows in his alcohol filled belly. He notices the strange lack of urgency in

Devries' voice, and wonders why he hadn't said all this when he talked to Frank at his locker after quarantine earlier in the evening. "What's all this shit about outside funding? And 'Have a pleasant evening'? That asshole! He can't just write off what that girl had as an *illness!*"

He remembers the way the girl had dived into his phlebotomy lab, her ropy veins extended to their limit all over her body, blood pressure obviously soaring. She crashed into Frank, and rushed back to the corner of his office as two doctors in scrub colors he didn't recognize came in through his door and closed it behind them.

As the girl passed Frank he smelled blood, an electric, copper penny smell, and a deeper, earthier smell, like damp topsoil. The intruding doctor with the dark hair said something like, "Please step back, sir." but Frank was too mesmerized by the girl in the corner to hear the request.

She was tearing herself apart. Her fingernails sank into the skin of her belly and tore upwards, leaving dark rivulets of torn matter. Her eyes were full of abject terror, and didn't seem to focus on anything, just flitted from left to right, up and down. They made contact with Frank's eyes for one second, and were full of pleading. Her eyes were screaming HELP ME! and Frank stepped forward to and was yanked back and placed in a stranglehold by the shorter intruding doctor. "Sir, you do not want to approach the patient. She is incredibly dangerous," said the strange doctor as his bicep flexed tighter into Frank's trachea.

Frank wanted so desperately to break free and help the girl, and he was attempting to shake loose and demand the two men help him when *it* happened. The young girl screamed, "THEY'RE IN-SIDE OF ME, GET THEM OUT! GET THEM OUT!" and was struck by some kind of seizure that flopped her back onto the floor, her head striking first and making a thick thud on the cold tile. Her back arched tight and blood bubbled from her mouth, running down the sides of her face, which then smeared with her sweat as she swung her head from left to right. As she arched her body her gown flopped back on to her face and muffled the gargling noises and panic filled grunts that her body forced out as she hemorrhaged. She managed to scream, "GET THEM OUT!" again and Frank had never been so afraid as when he saw what she was referring to.

He saw them then, hundreds of them, some kind of worm or parasite, snaking around just beneath the surface of her waxy white skin. She was seething with them. It looked like every inch of her body was crawling across her frame, all of her flesh in motion, and then Frank heard the sound, the sick tearing sound, and realized they were eating her, her connective tissues. These worm things were skinning her from the inside, eating everything that held her together, and Frank felt a sudden urge to vomit, and a stronger urge to run from the room, but he was still held tight by the man in the strange orange scrubs. Frank watched as the girl's skin grew loose as if she had aged a hundred years in ten seconds, the flesh of her face now slack and drooping anywhere the worms weren't moving beneath it.

She stilled and her back stopped arching and slapped wet to the tile and Frank thought that she was dead then but her body kept moving, shifting and bulging with the rapid snaking motions of the worms. One of her eyes, unencumbered by her drooping eyelids, pushed out onto her cheek, and Frank saw a mottled gray and pink worm slide out onto her face via the new hole.

The doctor guarding the door spoke in an almost jovial tone. "Rough cleanup, huh, Andolini?" He then stepped forward and pulled a spray bottle from a green pack that Frank hadn't noticed him carrying. He looked at Frank from the corner of his eye, never taking his sights off the twitching, boiling infestation on the floor. "Andolini, get that guy out of here. She's about to split."

As two rough hands pulled him from the room Frank saw the other doctor poised with his sleek aluminum spray can over the dead girl on the floor. She was bleeding from every orifice, and her skin began to tear open in hundreds of places, little gray and pink segmented worms spilling out, slick with crimson blood. Frank was jerked roughly into the hallway and heard the doctor still inside mutter, "Dear God..."

What the hell is going on?

It's Frank's ex-wife's voice again, inside his head, and he

resents the intrusion, but his rapid heartbeat and drunken confusion echo the sentiment. The contents of the day hit Frank with a unified impact, and his mind flashes over everything at once, his job, his loneliness, him nearly crying when he heard his daughter's voice, his ridiculous cleaning routine, his spontaneous liquor binge, the doctors in the orange scrubs saying "rough cleanup," and the girl, that poor girl being eaten alive from the inside. He had kept quiet about it, and just rolled right through quarantine without asking a single question, half of him feeling catatonic, the other half trapped in terror-induced denial. He tried to take Devries' suggestion and not think too deeply about it, but he had watched those little worms skin a girl *inside* in just a few minutes, and he didn't help her, he *couldn't help her...*

You could have helped her, Frank. You were afraid. So you watched her die and then you kept quiet about it for no good reason, and now you're diving into a bottle of booze. You wonder why we got divorced? Look at you. You're not a man.

Desperate to flush the voice out of his head, Frank turns away from the answering machine and makes a rush for the bottle sitting on the hutch. As he takes his second step forward he feels a strange, warm *shift* in his right ankle, followed by a pain so sharp he almost falls over from the white hot shock of it.

"What in Christ's name did I do there? I must have stepped on my foot at the wrong angle. My fault for staggering around like this," he thinks and he takes another step forward. He steps with care and as his right foot hits the carpet his ankle explodes in pain. His focus blurs until everything around him looks like it's underwater and he falls to the ground, almost unconscious from the razor sharp agony in his ankle. He cries out to the empty apartment and feels almost instantly embarrassed, somewhere past the immediacy of the pain. He gingerly pulls his right ankle in towards himself as he sits with his left leg splayed. He pulls back the cuff of his pant leg and expects another surge of pain. Instead he finds his sock soaking wet with blood.

"I'm bleeding. I'm *bleeding.* What the hell did I do to myself here?" he thinks, and as he reaches down and grabs the edge of his sock he prepares for the worst. The lights in his apartment flicker for a moment, throwing a tiny strobe effect on the floor that Frank mistakes for a drunken hallucination. He starts to roll back the fabric of his sock, which is now saturated with dark blood, and as he nears the base of his ankle he is struck by another shockwave of pain, this one strong enough to floor him. He flops back, unconscious as his head strikes the carpet with a muffled thud. As the wave of pain washes over and through and out of Frank he regains consciousness and feels a primal tingle in his extremities. He sits up slowly and waits for his pixilated vision to orient. For a moment he doesn't know where he is or how he got into his position.

The apartment is now pitch black.

Frank feels like he's at the bottom of a swimming pool filled with India ink. He can hardly breathe and his forehead is beaded with sweat. He hears another gust of wind whip through the street outside and realizes the storm must have knocked the power out. The thin crescent moon above sheds no light into skyscraper apartments, unless you have a penthouse.

"Great, just great! I got drunk, somehow broke my ankle, and now I'm blind," he thinks, with little humor. His heartbeat picks up as he surveys the situation. "I've got to get to my flashlight and see exactly what's going on with my ankle."

Frank orients himself in the murk and pulls himself over toward a small utility closet near his kitchen. He gasps and grinds his teeth as he feels another *shift* in his ankle, this one up higher than the last. "Why would the pain be moving up my damn leg?" he wonders, and the answer his subconscious formulates makes his heart palpitate closer to hummingbird speed.

Think about it, Franky Boy.

He feels the strange shift again and braces himself against another wave of pain, digging his elbows hard into the floor, clenching his abdominal muscles, and when he is content the pain has subsided he continues crawling towards the closet. Once there he pulls the thin door open and reaches into the back of the closet and grabs a bag containing his camping equipment. He digs into his neon orange duffle bag and pulls out most of the contents. At the very bottom he finds what he is looking for. He clicks the small rubber button and his Maglite glows bright on the camping debris around him. A parka, a butane torch, two pieces of Readystart kindling, an unfrozen packet of Blue Ice, a small hatchet, a wooly knit hat, a bungee cord, and a large First Aid kit.

He swings the light onto his ankle and very carefully pulls his foot in closer to his groin. His ankle is burning now and he winces as he pulls the cuff of his pant leg back. His sock is sodden with blood. Frank's stomach curls over on itself and threatens to divest itself of its contents. Frank has been living with blood, often sixty hours a week, at the lab, but the sight of his own still makes him feel very small and fragile. He grimaces and pulls the sock back, expecting to see a jutting shard of bone sticking out, figuring a compound fracture would be the only thing that could hurt this much.

Just beneath his inner right ankle, oozing blood, is a perfectly round hole, about the circumference of a pencil. Frank's heart squeezes tight and doesn't release for three seconds, and he struggles, gasping to pull in fresh air. "Now how do I manage to get a puncture wound and not feel it for so long?" he says. Speaking out loud doesn't provide the comfort that he thought it would.

Open your eyes, Franky boy. You brought your work home with you.

That was the phrase Frank's wife used at the divorce hearing. "He brings his work home with him, your Honor. He internalizes all his work stress and brings it home with him and my daughter and I have to deal with his mood swings and tantrums. ... No, he's never threatened either of us, your Honor, but you should see the look in his eyes after a long shift. ... No, he seldom has time for myself or my daughter. ... Yes, sir, he was a stable provider, but if that was all I wanted I would have married Amish." Frank had been stunned when the judge laughed aloud. "Yes, sir, he just values his job more than he values his family."

Frank sits on the floor in a state of disbelief, wondering how the hell he got to exactly where he is now. He knows that thinking about his divorce is morbid and pointless but he is growing more horrified by the second as he looks at the *too perfect* hole in his ankle, and he finds sadness somehow more comforting than terror.

He can barely get his hands to stop shaking long enough to unclasp the metal latch on the old First Aid kit. He opens the box and pulls out a few swabs, a small bottle of alcohol, a pair of scissors, a gauze pad, and a scalpel that he had co-opted from his graduation at Penn State. He holds the Maglite in his mouth, and his breath rolls out rapidly around its metal base, hot and stale. He shifts his body to the right so that his leg rests on the tiled kitchen flooring, and he pulls the plastic parka underneath it to keep the blood from staining the ground.

His teeth press tight against the flashlight almost to the point of chipping as he wets a swab with alcohol and prepares to clean the wound. "Hold on," he thinks as he pushes the swab down around the bleeding hole. The sting is instant, but nowhere near the sudden shock he feels when he sees motion beneath his skin. He thinks it is a vein at first, shifting as his foot moves, but then he realizes that no vein wraps around the ankle in a perfect circle.

There, beneath his skin, pulsing to a separate beat than Frank's veins, is a small protrusion. The skin circling his ankle is loose and something thick and warm is moving slowly under the surface.

Frank is sitting still but nearly vomits as his stomach takes a roller-coaster size drop. He blinks to clear his sight, and moves the flashlight in closer. There is no doubt. Something foreign is under Frank's skin, and it is making progress up his leg.

Inside his head he hears the girl screaming.

GET THEM OUT!

Frank panics, heart racing, and strips off his shirt to check out his skin. His hands rush around the surface of his skin, crawl over his face, and he points the Maglite where he can, and he wonders how many are inside of him, right now, chewing away at the things that hold him together, unstitching him, eating him. He pulls his shoes off and throws them over his shoulders. One of them topples a glass vase with some old dried flowers in it, and it shatters as it strikes the floor. Frank barely notices. His panic becomes overwhelming as he strips off his socks and checks his feet.

"If there were any more of those things in me right now I'd feel them," he hopes, thinking of the intense pain that this one small visitor is causing him.

There is another shift as the warm, soft intruder begins to move up towards Frank's calf, and the pain hits him in the belly, and Frank turns his head to the left. This time he can't hold back and the night's booze gushes out of his mouth, the Maglite falling to the floor with the deluge. "Whatever this thing is doing under my skin, it's toxic." His heaving subsides.

Do something, Franky boy.

A bolt of adrenaline singes Frank's nerves and he finds himself very anxious to get this *thing* out of his body before another wave of that sick gutfire pain hits. He remembers seeing the girl tearing away at herself with her own hands. Oriented by the adrenaline, Frank decides to proceed in a more civilized manner. He reaches down and picks up the alcohol swab and the scalpel and turns to his left and picks up the wet Maglite and puts it back between his teeth. He brings his right leg close again and swabs the area just above the intruder, and as he brings the scalpel closer he wishes both that he had never drank that evening and that he were much more drunk.

The paradox of self-surgery, Franky. How do you stay alert and steady while anesthetized? Can you, Franky? Can you even do this? You couldn't save our marriage, can you save your own life?

Frank feels like yelling "Shut up, you bitch!" but realizes there's no one in the apartment but him.

The slow pulsing movement of the parasite chewing its way up the inside of Frank's leg pulls him back into focus and he pushes the scalpel into the skin just above the worm's path. Frank is so flooded with endorphins that he barely feels the metal blade slice into his skin, creating a ten centimeter wide cut through every layer. He sits and stares, repulsed as the worm moves closer to the hole, intent on its path. Sweat drips from Frank's forehead as he reaches over and grabs a cheap, tarnished pair of tweezers from the First Aid kit.

He sees a tiny movement in the wound he has spread open and watches as the worm's head comes into view. It is grayish pink in the few spots that aren't slick with blood, and at the head, where Frank expects to see tiny, razor sharp teeth, he instead sees a thin white mucus being secreted from the mouth of the worm. Frank has never heard of a parasite that actively melts its host's tissues with a secreted acid, and he's watched a lot of Discovery since the divorce.

"Someone made this. Why in the hell would someone make this?" he thinks and is fascinated and disgusted at the same time as he moves the tweezers in towards the head of the worm.

The worm seems to sense the tweezers as they approach, and it retracts itself a bit, the motion sending bolts of pain through Frank's leg, like white phosphor burning under his skin. He seizes on the pain and pushes the tweezers in deep and clasps them down when he finds purchase. He has the tweezers an inch deep into the wound and they are clamped tight around the soft body of the worm.

The worm ruptures.

Frank swiftly pulls the tweezers out to discover they are holding onto only half of the worm, its thick gray pink segment still twisting above the metal. He pulls the segment closer to the flashlight and has to look at it almost cross-eyed to focus. He sees then the nature of the parasite, and thinks, "This is how I am going to die."

Inside the twisting segment clasped in the tweezers, just beneath the near translucent skin of the worm, Frank sees *them*. The babies. The thousands of tiny worms inside the larger one. The big one's just their mother, the delivery system.

He can feel them, the army of tiny worms squirming loose from the torn carcass of the large one, and he realizes that this is what happened to the girl. They get under your skin, find a nice place to rest, and then they burst, and the thousands of newborns tear you to pieces, inside.

He internalizes his work, your Honor.

Frank feels a moment of nothing. He has never felt so empty and alone, hopeless and ready to die. Then, as the pain in his leg starts to spread like quicksilver, two sentences echo in his head, spurring him to action. He hears the voices of two girls.

The first voice screams, the sound of the violated.

"GET THEM OUT OF ME!"

The second voice speaks, the sound of love.

"I can't wait to see you again, Daddy!"

Driven by an animal level desire to survive, Frank reaches for the kindling hatchet that he had pulled out of his camping bag. He sits there, watching his leg seethe and squirm beneath the surface, and hesitates for one second before bringing the blade down on his leg just above the knee.

The first swing of the blade flays his leg wide open, exposing subcutaneous fat and the meat of his muscle. The second swing strikes marrow, and for a second the blade hesitates to release from his femur as he jerks it back up for another blow. The third swing shatters bone and tears all the way through his leg. The blade sticks into the floor beneath him.

He grabs the wooly knit hat in one hand and the butane torch in the other and pushes himself ten feet away from the remainder of his right leg, leaving a thick gout of blood behind him. He presses the cap onto the stump and tries to staunch the flow from his vast wound. He is in shock and his blood pressure goes dangerously low as he ignites the butane torch. Acting on his last reserves of strength he pulls the soaking wooly knit hat off of the stump and turns the butane torch to the wound, knowing that he's more likely to survive a third degree burn than total blood loss.

He has never known such pain. His body is overcome with throbbing, absolute pain, pure as fire, and he stays in motion only by will and adrenaline.

He has never felt so alive as he does in each moment of this that he survives.

He drags himself over to the twitching, decimated leg in the kitchen and places the flame of the butane torch to the hive that was once part of his body, setting his Readystart kindling on each side of it.

As he watches the leg burn down to the blackened tile and

hears the soft boiling sound of the worms bursting he feels shock settle deeper in. He thinks, "Mr. Devries, I hereby tender my resignation," and doesn't recognize the sound of his own voice, laughing.

Frank wants to live, and does what he can to survive. He tries to care for his wound as he prepares to leave the smoky apartment. A small blanket off the back of his couch is wrapped around his stump and secured triple tight by a bungee cord acting as a makeshift tourniquet. A handful of vicodan allow him to move in spite of the crippling pain. A varnished cypress walking stick with an ornate lion's head handle keeps him from toppling.

As he leaves his apartment he grabs his hatchet, wipes it clean, and tucks it into the waist of his pants. He also collects his keys, his wallet, his hidden stash of large bills totaling four thousand dollars, and a small note with an address and a phone number on it which sat on a roll top desk near the foyer.

He carries the hatchet in case the escort Mr. Devries mentioned is waiting outside of his building. Mr. Devries, who wanted Frank to keep quiet. Mr. Devries, who had access to Frank's locker, and knew about the parasites. Mr. Devries, who hadn't been worried about Frank talking to anyone because he didn't expect Frank to see the dawn of the next day.

He carries the cash so he can bribe the first taxi driver he sees in the aftermath of the storm to take him to a hospital three counties away, where Mr. Devries can't find him, at least not right away.

He carries the note so he can call his daughter from the hospital and tell her he has some unexpected time off from work.

PRIAPISM

I really think this lecture is warranted, Ron. Actually, don't think of it as a lecture. Let's not set up some sort of teacher/student dynamic, when it's both of us that should be learning from what you have been doing. I mean, I know exactly what I'm talking about here, so I suppose I'm not actually learning anything, but I just don't want you to think I'm condescending you. I have always tried to treat you as an equal Ron, regardless of our age difference and familial relationship. On the inside you have an intellect, and while it may not be as finely honed as mine, it must be respected. Intellect must be worshipped Ron. It, and the opposable thumb, and maybe nuclear power, are the only things that save us from spending all day crawling about in the woods, foraging for berries and biting into boars with our little incisors.

Consider that a rhesus monkey one third my weight has muscles that are five times stronger. It's my intellect versus his muscles. Look who won, Ronny! Of course our intellect saved us. The rhesus monkey is now relegated to carnival work, and in some cases, the care of quadriplegics. How's that for the victory of the mind? A little cerebellum in the skull and you can make vicious, fetid animals serve and wipe the asses of invalids.

I'm trying to establish a respect in you, a respect for the power, the immense force that your mind can wield. As I was saying, even when you were in your crib, mewling and shitting your plastic diapers, I respected the mind that I knew you had. I read to you each night, fine works by Plato, and Pynchon, and Joyce, and I think maybe you understood. You had a look in your eyes when I was reading to you, although it was always post your evening breast feeding, so that look may have just been a symptom of gas. Or perhaps, as I believe, it was a combination of gas and understanding. Yes, that was it. You were tiny, but your mind was stewing to a head as swiftly as your bowels.

Oh, forgive my scatological way of speaking. I suppose by speaking in such a way I only hurt the thoughts and ideas I wish to serve. Ron, you must learn that ideas can be greater than the man who thinks them. Ideas are the finery we wrap our brains in, to try and hide the reptile core that we can't escape. The reptile brain, Ron, is a vestige of the past that we can't seem to slip loose of. We chug-chug-chug towards the future, and the world of ideas grows exponentially, but we are still base creatures at times. We all have those sad, tragic moments where we neglect thought and act on old, withered snippets of instinct.

Ron, never respect instinct. Look where instincts got the manatees. Every year, without thinking, they return to the same waters so they can be Ginsued to bloody shreds by my new outboard Yamaha motor. You remember how we always used to go to Florida? Killing those manatees was not just good fun, it was a statement, a bright red example of the superiority of man's intellect. It's a seamless statement really. There I am, with my loving nuclear family, sitting in a creation of man's genius, of man's hard work, and will, and intellect. Thanks to the mind, Ron, we were capable of attaining great speeds over an environment that humans have always found threatening, and as a result of our actions, those creatures controlled by instinct, by mechanical synaptic triggers, incapable of truly thinking, incapable of writing an immaculate Haiku, incapable of speaking five languages, those dull creatures were destroyed.

We survived, we enjoyed and consumed. We Goddamn transcended! We were in control!

Ron, you know your Dad can get a little passionate about things of this nature. Right there, right there, that's it though, Ron. That duplicitous mixture of physical passion and intellect, that's where you have try and keep your self. That's where the genius comes from. Like Amadeus, he had the intellect, but until he felt the wave of beats and sound against his head, with his head on the piano, that's when the genius happened. That mixture, Ron, once felt, is something you can really believe in. Then you search for it, and the more you search for it, the closer you get to the brilliance of your self.

Ron, we really do need to address what you have been doing with yourself. You mother recently brought to my attention that you have been violating yourself.

Masturbation, Ron.

Now I can see by the blood in your cheeks that this is true. I had hoped that your mother was misled, but now there's no doubt. Ron, you are fourteen, so I don't expect you to be engaging in sexual relations yet, and I'm certain you feel certain needs, but there has to be a better way of expressing those desires. Masturbation has nothing to do with thought Ron, absolutely nothing to do with the intellect that I have tried to instill in you. It is a simple case of stimulus and response. Oh, I'm certain the mind comes into play at times, when your body needs some sort of stimulus maybe the mind has to create a fantasy, but that sort of thing doesn't really count.

Worse yet, your mother has had to clean up for your filthy behavior. Your effluvia have managed to clog up the shower twice, and while in a certain way I can admire your raw physical tenacity, this is really just disgusting. Not thoughtful at all. Great men do not jerk off, son. Great men take that sexual tension which is now budding inside of you, and they control it. They subvert it.

Try and look at any great achievement of man and not find repressed sex, sublimated wants and needs. Pyramids, the "breasts" of mother Egypt, the music of Strauss, rife with sweat and lust, and look at skyscrapers for God's sake. Nothing is a more obvious phallus than a skyscraper. That no architect ever had the honesty to attach some sort of testes to his building surprises me.

So, Ron, I need you to stop defiling yourself as soon as possible, and stay out of our room especially. Your mother's high heels are never to be touched again!

You must be wondering what your punishment is Ronald. I don't always see justice in parental punishment, and I would prefer to think that we could simply confer, mind to mind, and that would be that, but in this case, when your behavior involves such a gut wrenchingly simian action, I feel that the punishment needs to be more direct, more Skinner-esque. And I cannot forget the immense effectiveness of my father's own methods, upon discovering me with one of his cigars. Smoking the lot nearly killed me, but I learned, damn it. I learned.

So, young man, now the time is at hand, pardon my dubious pun.

You are going to masturbate non-stop for the next five hours, while I play the complete works of Kenny Loggins on your mother's piano. I can't think of any other music less erotic. You will have no lubricant; you will have no stimulating reading materials. You will not be allowed near any shoes. You are to go over into that bare corner and sit on the rough wooden floor, and you are to whack it for an immense duration of time. If your penis becomes flaccid, you must continue pumping. If you begin to bleed, then you may have a styptic pencil for sealing the wound, but this is the only concession I will grant you. Whenever you have an orgasm you must pray to your own intellect to forgive you. You must say to your mind, "I am sorry for being a dirty ape!" At the end of these five hours you will be put directly to sleep, regardless of the loss of fluids, proteins, and electrolytes. When you awake in the morning you may have sore genitals and extreme forearm fatigue, but you will be a better, brighter person. Perhaps you will even become a man, it can happen just like that, when you finally take control of your mind and your life.

I am going to grab some vermouth and my Kenny Loggins sheet music, and I think you should get into the corner right now. I will let you know as soon as I am ready to begin your healing. Tomorrow,

Ron, you'll thank me for this, but for now we begin our descent into the beast.

Whip it out, son; it is time to make some repairs to your mind.

LUMINARY

My brother burned to death in the summer of 1967. The doctors never found any evidence of the fire on his flesh, any scar on his skin.

I know the truth. I watched him burn.

My brother's name was Martin Tally. I called him Marty.

Marty was a young man prone to daydreaming, and had a distant quality that strangers mistook for carelessness. Those who spent any significant time with him could identify his drifting eyes and long moments of silence for what they really were- an intense thoughtfulness, the focused kind of calm needed to contain boundless energy. His deep brown eyes, often hidden below a furrowed brow, seemed permanently etched with question marks. At moments of understanding his eyes shone with blazing exclamation points.

His eyes were full of light the day he tried to explain the human body to me. He rattled off Latin words and the names of bones and tissues and organs until he was almost breathless, concluding with, "You and me, Petey, we're the most magnificent machines ever built." Then he laughed, this deep laugh, and he seemed to marvel that the sound was coming from his own body.

His eyes were on fire when he took me up to the roof of our one-story house to watch the stars fall. He ushered me up our rickety wooden ladder and came up behind me, carrying three blankets, two cans of soda, and a pack of saltines. We sipped on our sodas and crunched our crackers until we were covered with crumbs and giddy from the sugar and we watched the night sky produce star after star. He had heard about an expected meteor shower, and laughed as he saw the first stone streak fire in a straight line towards the Earth. We watched for two hours as flaming rocks painted the sky with thin brushstrokes, our silence punctuated by the occasional sound of his laughter.

Towards the end of the meteor shower I turned onto my side and watched him watching the sky, his eyes shining. As if he could sense my eyes on him he said, "Pete, I know Mom didn't raise us churchy, but I want you to always remember what you saw tonight, okay, Bud? 'Cause that, that up there, what we just saw, is proof of God."

My brother's eyes were ablaze the time I got caught skipping school with Percy Brewston and Mark Bowling, and tried to shift the blame to my friends. I said, "Well, it was Mark's idea and I just thought..."

Marty didn't give me time to finish the sentence. "If it was Mark's idea then you didn't think anything, you followed. At least Mark had an idea, and he acted on it. You had no idea what you were doing. You acted without the conviction of you own decision, and now you have to suffer the consequences. Lemmings follow, Pete, and men think."

At the time I didn't even know what lemmings were, but from the sharp glint in his eyes I knew that it was far better to be a man.

I learned most of the lessons I still consider valuable from Marty, who, although only seven years older than me, was the closest thing I had to a father.

The real deal, the biological Pops, was a door-to-door sales-man who Mom said became a door-to-door husband, rendering the service for women in need. After spending days looping through mi-crofiche at the library, I discovered that Pops' final sale was closed at a house in Cronston, Ohio where he was caught rendering his hus-bandry service with the wife of an infuriated carpenter. It turned out that the carpenter had enough energy for a little overtime, and a hammer to the face ended my father's illustrious career.

I didn't need my dad. Mom kept me warm and kept food in my belly. My sister Vanessa made me laugh. Marty taught me about science, and math, and writing, and during the summer of 1967 he taught me about miracles.

Marty was seventeen years old, I was ten, and Vanessa was five. We were all old enough to know something was seriously wrong with our cat, Teddy. Teddy had taken to pissing freely anywhere he felt like losing some fluids. He also maintained a Rip Van Winkle-esque sleep schedule, surprising for a cat that used to spend all hours chasing invisible antagonists and terrorizing birds in the acreage near our house.

One afternoon I found Teddy resting on his side in the front yard. He was mewling just loud enough for me to hear through the screen door. His furry chest was matted with sweat, and was barely rising with his breath. His head was resting in a small, dark pink pool of his own vomit.

I didn't expect Mom home from her job at the cannery for another three hours, and I couldn't leave Teddy lying there in that condition, so I went and knocked on Marty's door.

I never knocked on Marty's door, especially after school. Marty tended to cloister himself away for long periods of time, focused on his books and his beloved chemistry set, and he didn't take well to interruptions. The last time I had interrupted him it had taken me twenty minutes to un-lodge the resultant wedgie. Still, Teddy appeared to be knocking on death's door with both paws.

Marty appeared at the door. "Aww, for Christ's sake, Petey, don't bother me. Go play with Vanessa or something. I have reading to do!"

I peeked past him and scoped out his always Spartan room, the small bed, the neatly kept wooden desk with the small desk lamp, the toddler-size stack of text books by his bed stand.

Tears welled to the surface. I sobbed, "Marty, you gotta see Teddy!"

Moments later we were in the front yard, crouched over the gaunt and barely breathing cat.

The question marks had entered Marty's eyes, and I watched him watch Teddy, breathing calm as he softly stroked the cat's head. He turned to me and said, "Bring me a blanket from your room, one you don't mind not getting back."

I ran to my room and grabbed an old, ratty, yellow blanket that made my skin itch upon contact. I ran back and presented it to Marty, who was whispering something to the cat that sounded like, "It could work, Teddy. It could really work."

Marty used the blanket to clean the vomit away from Teddy and then pressed the fabric across his palms and scooped his hands softly under the cat's neck and hindquarters. He wrapped the rest of the blanket around the body of the cat, who had stopped his sad mewling.

Marty carried the cat to his room and shut the door. I heard the lock tumble. I panicked and ran to Marty's door and was about to yell, "What the hell are you doing to our cat?" when his voice came calmly from the other side. He said, "Pete, listen very closely. I am going to fix Teddy, but it's going to take me a few days, and I'll need your help. We can't tell Mom about this because she'll want to take Teddy to the vet, and they will want to kill him. They don't know what I know, or at least what I think I know, and I think I might be Teddy's only chance to live. Petey, will you swear, on Teddy, and God, and everything, that you won't tell Mom?"

"Yes, I swear."

For the next few days I played coy, suggesting to Mom that Teddy might have run away. She seemed less concerned than I expected. I guessed that three kids and a full time job was enough responsibility without having to worry about the disappearance of our incontinent cat.

Each night I asked Marty what was happening and each night he offered no answers, instead insisting that Vanessa and I follow him out into the rolling fields near our house.

Each night, for six nights in a row, the three of us walked into the field during the soft light of dusk and caught fireflies. Marty supplied us with bug catching nets and jars with metal lids that had holes punched in the top. We swung our nets through the air and captured the little flickers of light that buzzed around us. We coerced the glowing luminescent beetles into our jars, where they grew frantic and flickered even faster.

While we were in the field Marty taught us about our tiny prey. We learned that the males flashed every five seconds, the females every two. Vanessa laughed and devoted herself to catching only the fastest flickering of the bugs. We learned the fireflies came from the family Lampyridae, which I remember only because it has the word "lamp" in it. Marty said the beetles made light out of two chemicals, luciferin and luciferase, both named after Lucifer, the angel of fallen light.

Each night Marty took the bug filled jars from us and locked himself away in his room, occasionally appearing in the kitchen to grab a bag of cat food or some ice. Every once in awhile I would see a light green glow coming from beneath Marty's locked door.

Things disappeared from around the house.

The fourth day after Teddy collapsed I noticed the absence of several items, most notably a card table, a small wooden chair, my mother's razor from the bathroom, and my father's old insulin injection kit from the medicine cabinet. It made no sense at the time, and I began to doubt Marty.

The seventh night after Teddy fell ill, my sister disappeared.

My mom had set out dinner, meat loaf with onions and mashed potatoes, and she called for us. Marty and I arrived at the table, but Vanessa was nowhere to be found. We walked the perimeter of our small residence. Marty noticed that the fireflies were out early that night. The exclamation points sparkled in his eyes. He ran to our tool shed, with me trailing behind.

Marty threw open the doors of the shed and gasped, "Oh, shit, Petey, she went firefly hunting without us."

There were only two insect nets hanging up in the shed.

We ran back to the house and grabbed Mom, explaining to her about our nightly trips to the field to gather the glowing insects. She asked "Why?" and Marty offered no answer. He was too intent on getting to the field and finding Vanessa.

We trudged through the field as the sky grew darker, ever blacker. I felt my heart drop into my toes and my stomach rise to my throat when I heard Vanessa's voice, screaming somewhere far away. We followed the sound, the three of us, now running, and I skinned my knees when I tripped on a downward slope in the field.

I looked behind me and saw the third insect net lying on the ground. Where the hell was Vanessa and why would she drop her net? My body was instantly soaked in sweat and my mouth dry as a tomb. I felt sick to my stomach but held the gorge back as Marty and my mom rushed towards the sound of my sister's faint screams.

We found Vanessa on the far southeast end of the field, in the area just before a jutting line of trees at the edge of the thick and boggy marsh. She was trapped under a collapsed deadfall of old, heavy whisper oaks. We could see her little arm sticking out, torn with scratches. What I could see of her body was either incredibly pale or bleeding. Worse than that, she had stopped screaming as we reached her. There was no comfort in that quiet.

As my mom reached forward to grasp Vanessa's hand she pushed aside a thick branch and the deadfall shifted. Trees crackled and smashed through each other, pinning Vanessa deeper and pulling a desperate scream from my mother's throat.

In the growing darkness I saw the metal in Marty's eyes, the calm and the wisdom beyond his years. He said, "It's going to be okay. No one move, any motion and those trees could collapse further. I am going back to house, and when I return things are going to be okay."

My Mom and I stood silent. I felt a sudden calm as I watched Marty run up the field, his legs graceful beneath him.

The blanket of darkness dropped over the sky.

I agonized over each second that passed without Marty's return. Each moment slammed into me, heavy and punctuated like the heartbeat of a giant.

I saw Marty first, out of my peripheral vision, and then my Mom saw him. "Look..." she said. Light filled our senses. Marty ran towards us at an incredible speed, streaking a sharp green light behind him. As he got closer to us, about halfway across the field, I could tell it was no illusion. He was glowing, bioluminescent. Tiny fireflies rose from the floor of the field and circled him, like planets orbiting the sun.

Marty's veins were on fire, glowing bright green. Every artery, every twist and turn of his body that blood flowed through was emanating a blinding light, and his eyes were absolutely saturated with it. The whole field within thirty feet of my brother glowed like daylight. The left side of his chest was shimmering, too bright to look into where his heart was circulating the liquid fire of his blood, so filled with light that his chest had become translucent.

We watched him then, stunned.

We watched as he lifted the mass of shattered trees that hung over my sister.

We watched as he reached one glowing arm into the deadfall and gingerly eased my sister's broken body out and placed her at my mother's feet.

We watched as the deadfall finally crashed in on itself, splintering, sending shards of old wood flying around us.

We watched as my brother, his flesh on fire, pulled one of my father's old insulin syringes from his pants pocket and slid it into his femoral artery, drawing blood. The blood shone so bright in the glass syringe that I couldn't look at it directly. He carefully placed the needle in Vanessa's left arm, at the bend, and depressed the plunger. Her breathing became steady, her color returned, and a faint glow came from her veins.

Marty spoke to us. He said, in a voice amplified with a strange, buzzing undercurrent, "*Vanessa's going to be all right. I must rest here for a moment, but you need to get Vanessa to a doctor right away. I think she's bleeding on the inside. I love you so much, and I know you love me the same, so you have to trust me, and go now!*"

My mom and I rushed Vanessa back to the house. I ran inside and grabbed a thick blanket off the back of the couch, which we used to keep Vanessa warm on the way to the hospital.

Mom and I remained silent the whole time Vanessa was with the doctors, both of us floating in a strange sort of daze, knowing we'd just witnessed something incredible, maybe impossible.

Later, when Vanessa had stabilized and we returned from the hospital, I ran around the house looking for Marty, searching for that bright glow. I found him in his bedroom, lying under his covers.

His chest did not rise or fall. His light, which hours before had burnt itself into my retinas, was now extinguished.

As I walked over to Marty and crouched down by his body I felt the first of a torrent of tears stream down my face, and hardly noticed the soft glow that had entered the room. It was Teddy, padding softly towards me and purring, his eyes glowing green.

I held onto Marty's body and cried until my Mom pulled me away and we called an ambulance. The medical technicians arrived and placed him on a stretcher to take him away. To them Marty looked like a boy, barely a man.

I knew what he really was. I held on to my mother as they carried away our fallen angel of light.

SATURN'S GAME

You could bite Todd's nose off.
That's the thought at the back of my head.
That's the thought I ignore. I squelch the sinister sentiment
and refocus on my friend.
Todd is saying this and that about motors and camshafts and
gear shifts and custom something, and the whole time I'm nodding my
head like one of those little plastic dogs people think add character to
their dashboard.
My eyes are focused on the little divot underneath his nose
where today's stubble is starting to grow, but I have these slick "Alien
Eye" Arnet sunglasses on and it's approaching sunset, so he can't tell
I'm not making eye contact.
Shadows are lengthening on the sidewalk in front of the coffee shop. My mind is wandering, making these electric connections,
chaotic. I'm thinking about the inadequate elastic in my sagging left
sock, the razor burn sting by my Adam's apple, the smell of barbe-
cued chicken in the distance, the cool edge that's creeping into the air.
I can't wait until Todd goes away, but I'm generally too polite to tell
people that they should not continue to interact with me.
The bad thought slingshots back into my brain, echo-heavy.
What if I grabbed Todd's head and then bit his nose off?

It's a poison thought, the kind of thing no one is supposed to think, or at least no one is supposed to *acknowledge thinking.* The thought came from a different part of my brain, and it feels like a misfire, a failed connection, a stillborn idea.

Still, what if?

Could I do it? Could I bite someone's nose off?

I'm trying to think something new but now I'm preoccupied with the idea of biting Todd's nose off.

I wonder if he's sensed the shift in my mentality, and how much danger he could potentially be in. I know I'm not supposed to think like this anymore, after the counseling with Dr. Marchand, but now the thought is looping, building speed, swirling down the brain drain.

It's a sick thought. Squash it, I'm thinking, it's just my frontal lobe fucking up again. If I do something crazy tonight, then Saturn wins.

He's been winning for twenty years.

Then the setting sun shifts one millimeter down in my field of sight, and one razor thin ray of light shoots directly into my optic cone and strikes the nerve like a match, and I'm overwhelmed by the smell of motor oil. Something...Oh God...and I look down and see a tiny green plant poking up through the crack in the sidewalk, and the plant sways a little bit in the breeze, and its motion blurs as it enters my eyes, and an electric jolt shoots up my spine and buries fire in my gut and I have to quench it.

So I grab Todd's head.

I've never bitten anyone's nose off before, but I figure that if I get a strong grip on the hair at each side of his head I could have a fair amount of leverage. From there, with the element of absolute surprise standing in my favor, all I have to do is open wide and clamp down.

My teeth sink through the skin of Todd's face after a split second of resistance and the teeth at the left side of my mouth crunch something. It might be that bony ridge at the top of the nose, or maybe the thin sliver of cartilage running down to its tip. Regardless of anatomy, it really crunches.

Todd is screaming now, his warm breath is right in my face, and his hands are at my wrists, trying to loosen my grip, but I'm too focused on the task at hand. I start to pull back as hard as I can, with my teeth sunk as deep as they can go into Todd's nose, and I tear my mouth downward at the last of it. The motion doesn't quite sever all the tissue so I have to make a couple of hard sawing motions with my incisors, like you have to do when you're eating sinewy flank steak. Todd's nose makes one last attempt to stay on his face before the wet tearing sound and the coppery taste in my mouth tell me I've succeeded.

Oh shit.

I just bit Todd's nose off.

It's in my mouth, and it is otherworldly warm, not a kind of warm that I'm used to. I spit it out onto the sidewalk where it lands with a moist plop. It looks fake, like it's made of rubber. It looks smaller than it did on Todd's face.

Todd is collapsed in a fetal ball on the ground. He's moaning, mewling, groaning, screaming, something. I can't quite tell. He doesn't sound good, and a crimson pool is spreading around his head.

Oh shit.

I don't think either of us expected this, Todd or I.

The view out of my sunglasses looks warped and liquid, distorted. A drop of Todd's blood is on the right lens, smearing its trail towards the ground. The sunglasses feel tight against my face, too tight, like they want to press into my skull and cleave the top third of my head off. It reminds me of the time when I was five and I got my head stuck in a plastic wastebasket. I tear the glasses off my face and throw them to the ground. My view feels instantly improved, my skull is safe.

I look back down at Todd.

One of Todd's Puma sneakers is unlaced, and I can still smell motor oil. My brain is buzzing, dull static numbing my ability to think. I've got to do something.

People will see Todd soon, police will come, medics will come. I'll be arrested.

I should just stand here.

My voice is falling out of my mouth and I sound all of twelve years old.

"Hey, Todd, oh fuck, Todd, I'm sorry, I'll just, um, wait, just..." I say to Todd, but he seems to be off in another world, and he's making these horrible moist, gargle noises. I'm confused. Static. Interference. Synapses are not connecting. I'm sniffing the air, inhaling deep, feeling like my nostrils are being coated with something dirty, black factory air. That thick industrial smell is saturating my head, covering my skin.

"Fucking motor oil! Can you smell it, Todd? The motor oil?"

I look down at Todd, who I think just said something like, "Gwaaaah, uunnaaa reggg, God, uhhh." Todd is definitely not smelling the motor oil.

I can't take the smell anymore. It's making my chest convulse, and I'm taking all these tiny excited breaths, like I'm trying to hyperventilate, only I don't want to, and my heart is beating so fast now that it's probably just vibrating, not even compressing, and I feel like passing out, my limbs are tingling, and I'm sweating profusely, drips rolling down my face, and so I just shake my head back and forth, back and forth, back and forth, fast and hard.

I'm trying to jar my brain into action.

I'm not dealing with this very well.

Todd's trying to stand up now, and someone just walked out the front door of Berenger's Pub across the street, and I can feel them looking at Todd and me. I can hear a Foreigner song coming out of the jukebox inside the pub. "Cold Blooded," I think, but I'm not sure. They all kind of sound the same to me. Songs do.

The man who just left the pub is looking at us now, and he's crossing the street. He looks kind of tubby, with big, meaty hamhock arms, and if he sees Todd like this he might think the wrong thing. He might think I did this on purpose. He might not know I have problems, and try to beat me up. I don't ever want to get hit again.

Now I am running.

Running to where?

Fuck it; I'm just running, pulse erratic, sweat streaming from every pore. I'm oozing sweat like a soggy sponge getting squeezed tight, positively soaking now, and my skin smells electrical. I'm still tasting Todd in my mouth. I have to run faster. Can I? My lungs feel like they are running at capacity and then some. My eyes are burning and I think tears are coming out, but I can't tell. It could just be sweat.

I'm about six blocks away from Todd and his severed sniffer, and I'm trying hard to run but it feels like someone just stuck a prison shank in my left side. Damage to the port side, Captain!

I'm heaving myself forward, trying to ignore the pain, laughing at my own little joke in short gasps, slowing down, trying to get some air.

Stop. Stand still. Breathe deep. Where can I go?

There's a defunct Sooper Saver-Mart to my left and a series of industry offices full of cubicles and small green plants to my right. I can see inside one of the cubicles, past my reflection in the glass. The lady who occupies the box has a tiny porcelain picture frame on her desk, and in the frame sits a photo of a house cat that looks like it might have eaten one too many servings of Atta-Kitty. A tiny, hand-written sticker on the picture frame says "MY GERGEN!" The lady has chosen *that* as her one tiny token of self in her uniform cube. A picture of a morbidly obese cat called GERGEN is her soul's little life-preserver, the one thing she has decided will save her from being sucked into the corporate undertow.

Maybe I'm not so bad off.

The Northside Liquor Store is only three blocks away from me. It is still open, and although I already feel sick and queasy I can't help thinking that maybe a huge bottle of rum is just the thing to make a bad, bad day turn better.

Prescription, Doc? 750 ml of self-administered distilled spirits should fix your malady, my good man!

I can already taste it on my tongue as I walk into the air-conditioned booze shop.

DING-DONG!

Oh, Holy Lord Jesus they've got their customer alert bell turned up loud. The store clerk turns to look at me and as he rotates I see a hearing aid manufactured at some point in the late Seventies is wedged in his ear. The thing is so gigantic that it looks like a beige octopus made out of plastic. It appears to be burrowing into his ear in an attempt to suck out his brains. He seems to pay the grotesque plastic apparatus no mind, which somehow makes it look all the more malevolent, like maybe it already got to him.

Then the old guy with the non-ergonomic and mechanically malicious hearing device says, "Hey buddy, stop starin' and buy something or I'll call the cops and report your ass for loiterin'."

Loiterin'. The worst of my crimes.

I hear him but aside from loitering I can't make much sense of the words. He seems antagonistic. My brain is turning increasingly fudgy, dense, and slow, and I'm thinking, Is he going to bite me?

I turn to my left and the wall trails by me in slow motion. Colors are blurring together like I did the wash wrong again. Things are not up to speed in my brain.

Another psychotic break, Doc?

I grab the first bottle of cheap, rotten rum that I see and boom up to the front counter.

I move forward so fast and so intently that the clerk shrinks back a bit. The strange and worried look spreading across his grill says he can't wait for me to leave. Can he sense I'm not right today?

The total bill comes to $14.56 and I've got a jug of shit rum in my left hand and a pack of Mini-Thins in my left pocket.

Pop pop fizz fizz-and I'm washing back cheap, legal speed with liquid fire.

Walking faster now, towards the park two blocks away, hoping to God that the shit I just swallowed will clear my head and help me to deal with this situation. Do I have a way out? Do I have to deal with this? Will they put me back in the fucking hospital? Can't I just see straight and fly right for once?

Too late, kid. Done is done, sport.

Yeah, and I'm pissed, feeling like this was never in my control. Blaming Saturn.

Your excuses won't reattach Todd's nose, will they?

The voice in my head is louder and now somehow not owned by me.

My insides are warming up, which is good because the sun is setting and the air will soon cool. Swigs off the bottle, two three four, in rapid succession, and now the world looks a little friendlier.

Then I hear the squelch and beep of a police car's radio, and everything seems ugly again. The air is alive with white noise and my eyes have static on their surface.

I look back over my left shoulder and see a black and white patrol car rounding the corner of Ward and Meeks. Adrenaline flushes through my system. My eyes burn. They've gone instantly dry. My throat fills up with booze and acid and I have to re-swallow, hard, to keep my liquid lunch from relocating.

Options: few to none. A voice at the back of my head is saying, "Stand very still. He will not see you if you stand very still." Fucking five-year-old logic, I can't escape it.

The cop car is closer with every split-second and my brain's not coughing up the goods.

Throw a rock at the car? Why?

Duck down, lay low? I'd look even more conspicuous if spotted.

Wait for the officer to get out of the car and get within biting distance, see if I can claim nose number two for the day? Low odds for survival, smashed in a locust-like swarm of lawmen.

Run?

Again? Well, it worked before...

I hear the bottle of rum smash to the concrete behind me and my legs are kicking doubletime. Crazy white heat is searing in my gut (this is all too much for one day) and I want to stop and throw up, but it's a fair bet that even if the patrol car wasn't looking for me before, they are interested in me now. They are awfully suspicious of people who flee their presence. They make assumptions. Draw conclusions.

I'm running down a thin alleyway now, taking in deep lungfuls of stale garbage stink, and I'm laughing like a kid. Oh boy, a chase! Only when I look over my left shoulder (Grandpa always told me I'd see Death coming for me over my left shoulder) all I see is the alleyway receding behind me. No cops. Maybe I am invisible, or maybe the cop was changing radio stations or looking at his fingernails or something else as I ran across the street. No trail.

No pursuit. *Deus ex machina* in my favor.

Especially since her house is only four blocks away.

I feel light in my shoes as my Mini-Thin engine goes into overdrive. I'm so close to a safe place, if she'll let me in. God, what an *If.*

Four blocks of footwork and three knocks on a pale red door connected to a cheap stucco apartment complex determine my fate. Will she or won't she let me in? Has she forgiven me? Will I find sanctuary or something much less pleasant?

The thin door creaks as it opens, and standing there in an old pair of Guess pajamas and an older pair of fuzzy white slippers is the sister I haven't seen for five years.

I'm speechless. I can't say a word. My lower jaw has dropped open on its hinge and I can't move my diaphragm or expand my chest or vibrate my larynx or make plosive sounds with my lips or anything. What do I say?

"Come in, I guess," she says as she turns slowly back towards the couch and the bowl of popcorn on it. "I'm watching this episode of Real World for the fourth time, but it's not getting any better. Don't ask me for money 'cause I won't give you shit. I'm barely making it as is."

One quick look around her place pins a verification on the statement. There are Salvation Army style blankets up instead of drapes, a broken down futon at the center of the room, movie posters on the walls (Switchblade Sisters, Reform School Girls, Bound etc.), cheap Target dishes, the anodized kind that stay almost ruthlessly cold, and stacked Ramen packets on the dusty countertop. Trailer park chic minus the porcelain unicorns and the "Hottest Men in Firefighting" calendar. Still, she let me in.

"What's up, Tyler?" she asks as she sits back down on the

futon and tucks a thin afghan over her lap.

"Um..."

Long pause. Beat...beat...beat...beat. I can't just waltz in here after five years incognito and tell her I'm on the lam because I just bit my friend's nose off for no good reason. "I was just in the neighborhood..."

"Bullshit, Ty. Fucking bullshit." She's still not looking at me, her eyes stay on the television, not blinking. "Ty, look down at your shirt. You fucked up again, huh?"

My shirt is plastered to me, the collar loose with sweat, and the front is saturated with crusting blood. My chest is a red waterfall that smells like moonshine. She's right, I most definitely fucked up again.

"First of all, Ty, if you're crazy again I want you to stay right where you are and understand that if you try anything I will pepper spray you until you choke on your own vomit. Second, I've heard the police sirens, and if you think I'm going to harbor you, well, you're crazier than you ever were. Well?... Talk, Ty, I'm not in the mood for games... listen, stop mouth breathing and tell me something. ...Say something, Ty, fucking talk. Habla! Stop staring at my wall and talk."

Shit, she's amped up and I'm slowed to a crawl. I'm terribly confused and I'm thinking they switched her Paxil to methamphetamine, 'cause I've never seen her this aggressive.

There used to be days when she wouldn't even get out of bed, she'd just lay there and stare at whatever was past the ceiling in her room.

"Sis, I'm scared."

"What'd you do?" she asks, but the undercurrent in her voice says she doesn't really want to know, that she's sick of this already.

"I... uh... well... there was this smell like motor oil, and the little plant was sending electricity to me, and I... well, I'm fucking sorry now, so sorry... and I think he's okay... things... I mean... I know what I did was... I know that I am sorry... I'm sorry, I'm so sorry and I really mean it... I'm so..." and then it's all too much for me and for the first time in weeks I'm really feeling something, and my breath is hitching and my knees are going weak and I'm sobbing as I hit the cracked linoleum and curl up on my side, and then the story spills out in between sick, wet sobs and snotsniffles, and tears so hot they feel like rubbing alcohol on my face.

I tell her about Todd's nose, and then his lack of a nose, and I tell her about the smell, the motor oil, and the angry man, and GERGEN, and the octopus eating the old man's head, and the booze, and the pills, and the panic, and somewhere in all of this mess I tell her that I miss her terribly, like everyday, and that I miss the way she smells. She kind of laughs and cries at that at the same time, and now she's getting off the couch, moving towards me.

She's standing above me now, looking down and mumbling something like, "Saturn's reign never ends, right?"

Saturn....

It's her nickname for Dad. I remember the first time I was in the hospital, she brought me this book of paintings by this Spanish guy, and on one of the pages there was this seriously fucked, black painting of the God Saturn chewing a big hole in his Son. Next to it was a Post-it Note that said, "Kind of reminds you of him, huh?" Ever since then, he's been Saturn.

Ever since then I've been playing his game. Trying to control myself, trying to deny what he did to me, trying to exist despite the scars on my brain that fucked up the wet-wiring.

Now she's crouching down over me and I *do* love the way she smells, like green apples, and I kind of want her to hold me, but I know she's going to blame him and talk about him now, and I'm sick of her treating our past like this great tragedy, because we are not a fucking heavy metal song, we are not a Goddamn Oprah Book-of-the-Month story, and we're not a made-for-T.V.-movie, and we don't have to be weak and afflicted like those people, like those songs and stories and now her arms are around me and I can tell that I'm shaking and she's rocking me just a little bit, just enough. She doesn't have to say anything.

Something switches inside of me and my brain kicks out some feedback and I'm smelling the dust embedded deep in the shag carpet in my bedroom, seeing the tiny droplets of blood that hung on the end of my eyelashes, hearing the sound of Dad snoring, passed out on the floor across the room, oblivious to what he has just done and already forgetting. I'm remembering the look on Mom's face when she came into the room and saw that the claw of Dad's hammer was buried in my skull.

What then? Doctor after doctor, surgical specialist, mental specialist, anger therapist, chemical dependency specialist, none of them explaining to me exactly how a Dad, a Buddy, can turn into Saturn and chomp down on his kid.

It's all noise now, right? He made his choices, I've tried to make mine.

Sis is kind of crying now, holding on to me. Maybe she's just shaking. She's so full of anger; I think maybe she took mine into storage when I got too crazy to deal with it. Yeah, maybe I am a heavy metal song.

So I'm curled up, and she pulls the afghan off the futon and drapes it over me, and I push my fingers through the little holes in the fabric and I try to make a cocoon, and I fall asleep there, with her running her fingers through my hair, the smell of green apples floating in between us.

...and when I wake up the first thing I see is blue and red flashing across my sister's plaster ceiling. I know she called them. Deep down I knew she would when I walked in the door. I'm not angry at her, she's just big on consequences, closure, whatever.

I'll go without conflict. They'll take me in and they'll call me a monster, and they won't be all that wrong.

They'll put me in the hospital. The staff will hear what I've done. They'll sweat fear when they stand near me. I'll try to prove to them that they're wrong.

Maybe I'll learn to control myself in there. I'll have the time. I'll practice. I'll try to focus.

For myself. For my sister. She'll visit. I know she will. Please, God.

There's a knock at the door.

I hope they'll let me take the afghan with me. It keeps away the cold.

I press the blanket up to my face, inhale very deeply, so that my nose and my throat are filled with green apples, sweet to bursting and wonderful. I close my eyes for a moment, open them, step forward, and open the front door.

BRANDED

The fucking mark. Raised, ropy-white and red-rimmed. A thick, knotty scar. Had it been a simple straight line, like an incision scar, I certainly could have moved beyond my revulsion. Love would have overcome and all that. Of course, this wasn't any simple incision scar. It was a fully 3-D scar that looked worse than the initial wound, and it was in the *exact* shape of the McDonald's logo. Goddamned Golden Arches! Only the scar was more sickly white than golden, and clean of any of the tiny, downy blonde hairs that rested near it. Upon first finding the scar, which was just to the inside of her right thigh, I laughed. AHA, so she tried to play a joke on me. A real josher, using prosthetic scars to gross me out. Ha-ha, very funny, now *TAKE IT OFF!*

One look in her eyes and I see that the scar is real, and there's no way in hell she wants to tell me about how she got it. Now she looks worried, like this is when the guys always bail out. I can't leave her, as much as my guts churn and threaten to spill out of my mouth. Plus, I'm stuck in a weird spot. To initiate a sort of deepening of our sexual relationship I had promised to go down on her. I mean, that's how I found the scar in the first place, when I was taking her shorts off. So there I was, nauseous and obligated to cunnilingus because I didn't want to be the millionth asshole guy in her life.

I closed my eyes as I began, trying to erase the image of the

Golden Arches scar. As my tongue separated labia and found the clit I suddenly saw Ronald McDonald behind my closed eyelids. As my tongue urged her on my brain was awash in all things McDonald's. Grimace and the Hamburgler, sizzling greasy beef being flipped with a scummy spatula by a pimple face kid whose pusy acne leaked yellow-red onto the skillet, smoking trails coming up off the beef and pus mixture, the killing floor for McDonald's Inc, where the blood and shit rushed from millions of Heifers as they mooed their last terrified moo, a boy covered in burn scars asking me if I wanted "fries with that," chickens shitting into six slightly similar McNugget molds, lick lick back and forth surging in to suppress my scar-induced nausea.

The more my tongue pressed the pink the more she began to taste like fancy ketchup. When she came she tightened her thighs and the scar pressed deep into my left cheek. For a moment I was marked too. I flinched. She noticed.

She was a wonderful human being, with a laugh that you'd want to hear at the gates of heaven.

And I am weak for leaving her.

THE SHARP DRESSED MAN
AT THE END OF THE LINE

He was collecting roaches. They moved faster than he expected them to. They'd be within centimeters of Dean's fingers and suddenly speed left or right with quarterback maneuverability. Crafty fuckers. Even more survival driven than he gave them credit for.

Survival, Dean's modus operandi. He understood the cockroaches on that level. Both of them had a clearly established Goal One:

Do Not Die.

He left out muffins. They swarmed the muffins. Dean harvested the unsuspecting bugs by the handful.

He replaced his regular bulbs with UV black lights, so he could see, but the roaches didn't scatter like they would under normal apartment light.

In between roach round-ups, he watched television. He grimaced. He cringed. Every image on the screen was a fat, flashing sign that read WW III.

The news showed Conflict with a capital C, international and senseless.

It caused Dean to sweat stress and stink up his flop pad, the worst in all of D.C. Check the rotting floorboards, the dripping faucets. Noise-aholic neighbor bass and baby screams as the soundscape. Swinging bare-bulb ambience. Mildew and asbestos fighting for airspace. Punctured pipes leaking slow into linoleum cracks. Plastered pellets of roach shit as the common denominator.

Living cheap. Barely living.

He watched television. The President poked angry bears with sharp sticks.

We will not relent to this Axis of Assholes!

Take that Iraqi-Bear!

They're hoarding weapons and plannin' rape missions!

Yield before us Korea-Bear!

Commie baby-killers, pure and simple!

Oh, China-Bear, you'll rue the day!

The President was up in the polls. The populace- petrified and war weary, but strangely supportive. Dean included. He'd back a bully… as long as El Presidente could guarantee a win. It was that possibility of a loss that spooked Dean to screeching simian defense levels. A loss, at this heavily armed and nuclear point in world history, meant Apocalypse.

Dean's answer- Cockroach Suit. Thousands of cockroaches hand stitched through the thorax, tightly sewn to a Penney's business suit bought on the cheap.

Dean's days and nights were occupied with the spreading of wings and the careful puncturing of his pathogenic pals with needle and thread. He positioned them all feet-out, so their mouths could still feed.

Dead roaches were of no use to Dean. The live ones carried the instinct.

The instinct had kept them alive for four hundred million years. Their bodies were natural radiation shock absorbers. They could live for ten days after being decapitated. Dean knew that in the event of Apocalypse, he'd be rolling with the right crew.

He knew they were training him for war, and for suffering. He'd already borne the brunt of their bacterial ballast. He'd coped with clostridium. He'd dealt with dysentery.

He was becoming impervious to disease, like them.

He kept and catalogued the roaches, separated into clusters of speedy Smokybrowns, ravenous Germans, and over-eating Americans.

Jars upon jars of the bugs were stored in his deep freezer. They slowed down in the chill. The cold goofed them like opium, kept them still.

It kept them from eating each other.

That insatiable appetite had been the primary problem with the first cockroach suit. Dean had left it out in the muggy tenement warmth at night, stored along with some chocolate cereal in a microwave-sized cardboard box. When he opened the box in the morning the cockroaches had not only eaten all the cereal, but had ravaged each other. His carefully crafted suit had gone cannibalistic.

He bought another suit. Dean didn't sweat his cash flow. Daddy Dean Sr.'s estate was still kicking out cash in steady intervals. The primary source of cash— royalties from the sale of Daddy Dean's Ivy League approved books on entomology.

Daddy Dean Sr. had been a big time bug man and serious scholar until his car accident. A deer had run into the road. Daddy Dean Sr. swerved hard with his right hand on the wheel. His left hand gripped a cherry Slurpee with a thick red straw. Daddy Dean Sr.'s car hit an elm tree straight on. The dependable airbag exploded and jammed the fortified Slurpee straw straight into Daddy Dean Sr.'s left nostril and right on through to his frontal lobe.

Dean had shown up at the scene in time to see the cops detach the straw and blood-filled cup.

Dean had heard one cop on the accident scene call it a "straw-botomy."

Dean didn't think it was funny.

Dean didn't think a single fucking thing was funny for quite a while, and resolved to find happiness however he could.

For a long while that meant spending Daddy's textbook royalties on hallucinogens. The "straw-botomy" had taught him that the world made no sense anyway, so he traveled the world hunting head-trips. He tongued toads. He feasted on fungus. He inhaled ayahuasca. A bad encounter with a sodomizing shaman and some industrial strength desert peyote finally scared Dean straight.

Then he moved back to the states and began his survival training.

He knew the world wanted to erase him. He'd seen it in visions. He'd seen it in the eyes of the priapic shaman. He saw flash frames of his own father felled by a plastic straw.

Dean moved to the slums of D.C. He wanted to move to a place that resisted and destroyed life. He knew there were survival secrets in the daily struggle.

He holed up and watched television. He watched El Presidente taunting nuclear armed countries anxious to see if they could one-up Hiroshima.

Y'all ain't got the bomb, or maybe y'all just ain't got the balls to use it!

C'mon Korea-Bear, show us you got a pair!

Dean read books about roaches. He studied sewing and stitch types. He bought spools of thread and heat sterilized needles.

Dean developed his cockroach suit and watched it fail.

He cried and sucked up the sick, musty attar of roaches when his first suit dined on itself.

He cursed himself when the second suit crawled through a hole in the crumbling apartment drywall. Fifty seconds to piss. That's all he'd taken. That was all they'd needed. He heard his roach riddled jacket and pants skittering around in the crawlspace above his kitchen.

Every time he failed, he felt as if Apocalypse was seconds away. He got weak, the blood flow to his head lagged. He thought he could hear the roar of approaching bombs overhead. He worked harder, his hands shaking with fear.

He ignored the doubt that crept into his skull and took up permanent residence.

Dean, don't you know the bomb is coming for you? You think some bugs and some cheap threads can stop a holocaust?

He ignored the fists that pounded on his door, the angry

screams, the vulgar notes slipped through the crack of his mail slot.

The note last Tuesday read: Mister room 308, you are the cockroach man and ever since you came all up in here they've gone crazy. My little sister has to wear cotton balls in her ears to keep them roaches from digging into her head and laying eggs, like they did with Brian. You ain't right at all Mister room 308, and you ought to leave and take your roaches with you. I see them coming out from under your front door right now. My dad says if Brian has eggs in his brain, then you die. Go away. Love, Maysie.

The neighbors thought Dean was bad mojo. They threatened litigation. They threatened worse. Dean knew it was part of the world's plan to erase him. He kept working.

Dean actually saw the first bomb hit. He knew it was coming.

He knew from the silence. El Presidente had gone quiet for three days. There were no more TV broadcasts promising patriotic retribution. There were no more shots on CNN of El Presidente grabbing his balls and shouting, "Eat this, Iran!"

El Presidente was quiet because he was hiding, somewhere, from the grief he saw coming America's way. El Presidente was crafty, even more survival driven than Dean had given him credit for.

In the calm before the atomic shit-storm, Dean finished his third cockroach suit.

It was perfect. A living tapestry of twitching legs and chittering mandibles. Add to the threads a pair of Kroeg blast goggles, a crash helmet, a refillable oxygen tank, and a thick pair of foil lined tan work boots, and Dean was suited up for survival.

When the first newscaster started crying on air, Dean suited up and began to walk from his apartment to the street. He didn't want to be inside that roach trap when the Earth started shaking.

Dean walked by apartments, heard the crying of the tenants. They could sense the bomb was coming. Their cries were weird, and strangely complacent, the mewling of doomed animals with no options. Baby seals, waiting for the spiked bat to spread their skulls wide.

It made Dean sad. He cried and fogged up his goggles. He felt the suit writhing around his body, taking in his warmth, seething. He stayed in motion.

Dean made it into the street and turned to his left, not sure quite where to go, hoping the cockroaches' instinct would take over soon. Then he would just lay down on his belly or his back and let them carry him to survival, like a God.

The D.C. streets were packed with people looking up at the sky, waiting. Dean expected chaos and conflict. No one even looked twice at him. They were waiting for the Big Delivery from above.

They got it, twenty seconds later.

The flash blinded Dean, even with the goggles and helmet on.

He crouched behind a cement stoop and heard the most cohesive and unified scream any dying species had ever let loose.

Then there was silence, and heat, terrible heat.

And, of course, darkness.

The cockroaches carried Dean, like a God. He woke to dark clouds and electrical storms overhead, and gray ash falling all around him. His retinas were blast burnt, but functional.

He was alive.

That was the part he could not comprehend.

He was fucking alive.

The roaches were too, and they were moving quickly towards a perceived food source. Dean felt them moving, swift and single-minded, driven by constant hunger.

His hands were cold. Nuclear winter was just beginning, and the air already approached frosty. He'd forgotten to buy gloves. He hunched his shoulders, pulled his hands inside the living suit. He relaxed and enjoyed the eerie quiet, and reveled in being alive. Being a survivor.

He moved without effort through the ash of nuclear winter. His suit surged beneath him as it crawled up onto a sidewalk. The legion of tiny legs pushed onward as Dean zoned out on the gray snowfall floating down from the sky.

He watched the sky turn darker. He saw thick red and green clouds of nuclear dust float above him. He saw an obelisk in the distance, stark and tarred jet black by the bomb blast.

It was the Washington Monument, just like he'd seen on T.V. There was something walking back and forth at the base of the monument. It moved like a human, but glowed bright yellow.

Dean let the suit carry him closer, and then stood up when he was within ten feet of the yellow shifting mass.

Dean lifted the visor of his helmet and de-fogged his goggles. He could see clearly after that, aside from the bright imprint of the blast that wouldn't leave his sight.

The peripatetic figure was a man. A man in a Twinkie suit. The thousands of Twinkies were half charred and oozing cream filling.

The man turned to face Dean.

The man's face was slack, and the eyes were empty of thought or feeling. Despite this lack of emotion, El Presidente was still the most recognizable man on Earth.

He looked at Dean and started to weep.

Dean opened his arms, offering a hug.

El Presidente stepped forward, and then hesitated. It was too late. The cockroach suit was upon him, a thousand mouths demanding to be fed.

Dean looked into El Presidente's eyes, caught dilated pupils, animal-level fear.

The eyes no longer promised Dean's destruction, as they had from the static screen of his television. The world's plan to erase Dean had failed; it was vaporized to dust, silt in sick Strontium-19 winds.

The scarred sky above Dean grew darker, the air around him even colder. Dean shivered; El Presidente screamed.

Dean reached up and warmed his hands around El Presidente's throat. He felt the pulse under his hands drop to zero.

The weeping had ended, and the feasting had begun.

TWO CAGES, ONE MOON

Karen had finally found a level of comfort in the trunk when Steven slowed the car and brought it to a rumbling stop. She had been so comfortable that the empty motor oil container lodged into her lower back didn't hurt anymore and had become a dull sort of presence. In contrast, the handcuffs that bound her were still causing discomfort, as they always did. "Nine months in these damn things and they still hurt."

She heard him rounding the car, coming to the rear with his keys jingling. She sucked down fresh air as he opened the trunk, knowing she wouldn't be out of the stale prison for long.

She was grateful that he took her out for her bathroom breaks, even if it was at his convenience. Within the first month after he abducted her from her studio apartment in Boise he had learned it was best to let her out every three or four hours. Karen now received less water and food than she used to for practical reasons. The urine smell had been heavy and floated from the trunk through the upholstery and eventually to Steven's nose whenever she emptied her bladder as a desperate measure. Steven had tried putting her in adult diapers, but Karen had developed a nasty rash and he hadn't like the way it looked or smelled. So, every three or four hours, if there happened to be a rest stop or gas station with bathrooms in the rear he pulled over and let her out for a few minutes.

Karen felt Steven's arms sliding under her back and the crook of her legs. He picked her up, grunting, and set her on the ground.

There wasn't anyone else at the rest stop. Karen thought Steven was very good at this, at keeping her, and he never stopped if there was someone that could spot them and see what he was up to. He was desperate to have her, to own her, and somewhere at the back of her head she enjoyed his need.

She held her hands out in front of her. It was part of their ritual. He inserted the tiny silver key and twisted it. He unlatched the cuffs and let her hands loose, knowing she wouldn't strike him or try to run. She had learned her lessons.

The first lesson was "Don't try to run." A blow to her head with his pistol had taught her this.

The second lesson was "Don't scream for help." A fist to her mouth had taught her this. Steven kept the two teeth she had spit out in his right pants pocket.

The third lesson was "Don't fight back." The thick razor scars in the webbing between her fingers had taught her this.

She was docile now, soft as a lamb. She had given up hope of escape after the first brutal week of her abduction.

He didn't hurt her anymore, not like he used to. She found she didn't fear him much, after a while. When he did hurt her it was usually quick and she found she was able to block out most of the pain. Her suffering, like any day-in, day-out routine, now bored her.

The full moons of each month still brought trouble, but other than that their relationship had become strangely placid.

Karen walked into the restroom. She enjoyed it as an oasis from the dark of her mobile prison. It was the only time she was ever alone, physically. Steven was waiting right outside the door for her, with the pistol tucked into the back of his pants, so she never felt free, but being out of the trunk and away from Steven for a few minutes was something she had grown to cherish.

She entered the stall and latched the door shut behind her. She dropped her underwear, the new, poorly fitting underwear that

Steven had purchased a few weeks ago, and rested on the cool porcelain with her elbows on her knees and her face cupped in her hands.

Karen saw the lipstick on the ground after she flushed, and until she grasped it she was sure it was a tiny mirage.

She thought for a moment about the content of her days with Steven. She thought about the beatings, and the trunk, the hot trunk full of stale air and rotten smells, and the dehydration, and the way that Steven would try to have sex with her and then hit her when he couldn't get hard, and she felt the anger in her belly turning to fire. She thought about the approaching full moon and wondered how many more cycles she could survive. She seized upon her chance and started writing with the lipstick on the beige wall of the bathroom stall.

She knew Steven would be getting impatient, and when he got nervous he got rough with her, so she acted swiftly, scrawling, "Help! Kidnapped! His name is Steven! We are in a burgundy Impala! Not a joke!"

She wanted to write more but the waxy lipstick ran out before she could get her own name on the wall. She tried to lift some excess lipstick from the message with her fingertips, but it began to smear beneath her shaking hands, and she gave up. She was a victim with no name, easier to forget and ignore.

Karen tried to act cool as she exited the bathroom. She had cleaned the makeup from her fingers and wrapped the lipstick container in half a roll of toilet paper and thrown it in the trash. She prayed Steven hadn't grown suspicious.

If he went into the bathroom and checked the stall, what then? She didn't believe he'd kill her, he needed her too much. Still, he could be cruel, and she didn't want to learn any more lessons at the edge of his razor.

She found Steven outside the door, looking at the palm of his hand where her two previously punched out teeth rested. He was looking at them with adoration. Love.

Karen held out her hands and felt the steel of the handcuffs bite into her raw, chafed wrists.

The next week passed quickly for Karen. She spent most of her time in darkness, cradled in the trunk of the car, sweating and sleeping, stirring through fever dreams. She didn't know what state they were in, but the air in the trunk smelled like onions. She didn't know what month it was, but she knew a full moon must be approaching because Steven had become very agitated.

A few months back Steven told Karen that the spirits he trapped in his blood chewed on his insides during a full moon. Steven was weird like that. Karen was fascinated by just how broken and disjointed his mind was, and often sympathized with him even though she didn't know how he had become so twisted up inside. There were hints, and glimpses of strange scars on his belly, but she never asked him questions. She feared the ugly answers would make her care about him (more than she already did).

Karen felt hope burning away inside of her, and passed her time wondering if anyone had seen her lipstick message. Did anyone believe it? Was the message too vague? Did some janitor wash it away? Would anyone call the police? Could she really be condemned to spend the rest of her life in a trunk, the carefully tended baggage of a lunatic?

Another full moon came and went, and the legion of deep bite marks covering the back of her legs throbbed and oozed. The biting was the only thing that calmed Steven down on a full moon. He fed her horse-size penicillin pills to keep the bites from getting infected, but she was allergic to them and broke out in hives. She was itching herself by rubbing back and forth on the rough carpet of the Impala when she heard the police sirens.

She felt the Impala speed up for a moment and she thought Steven might try to outrun the cop. Then she felt the car shake as it crested onto the rough shoulder of the road to stop.

Karen heard Steven yell to her, sternly.

"Don't say a word, not one Goddamn thing. I love you and they can't have you. Don't make me prove it."

Karen heard the crunch of the officer's boots on the roadway as he approached the car, and she pressed her head against the upholstery, straining to hear whatever she could.

Her heart beat was thumping in her head and she could barely hear a word over her own pulse and the idle of the boat-size car.

She heard both of their voices growing loud; Steven's taking on an incredulous and angry tone. She prayed Steven wouldn't shoot the cop.

Hope rushed through her whole body and she felt like screaming, "I'm in here! I'm in the trunk!"

The officer would save her and then she'd be free!

Free.

Free to return home to her thankless job and her overwhelming debt and her resentful kids that never called. Free to re-enter the dating scene as a scarred, forty-two-year-old ex-abductee. Free to fall asleep, crying and alone, between cold sheets. Free to be avoided and scorned. Free to be unwanted, unneeded.

Free to be alone.

She found herself silent, her scream for help stillborn as a sigh.

The concept of freedom, at the verge of its possible re-entry into Karen's life, became terrible. She found herself praying for the meddling police officer to go away. She pressed tighter against the back of the seat and heard Steven's voice.

"Yes, sir, absolutely, and thank you for pointing that out! I appreciate your concern!"

Later that night, while Steven carefully tended to Karen's bite wounds, he told her about the blown tail light on the Impala. They both laughed at their unexpected brush with the outside world.

As Karen drifted off to sleep she smelled iodine and felt it soaking into her wounds. The moon was thin outside, and her pain was at low tide. She found herself taking the strangest comfort in the fact that Steven kept her teeth in his pants pocket.

Such was love.

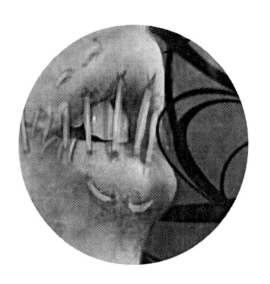

SPARKLERS BURNING

Martin set down the shoebox full of fingers that he was carrying to the kitchen and picked up the remote. He thought, "I've been working hard today. Why not relax for a moment and see who's talking on my box?"

The T.V. sparked on with a static crackle, shedding vivid light into the previously jet black room. Martin couldn't believe his luck. He thought, "I didn't even have to flip no channels and there you are. Yes, yes, yes, there you are."

The perfectly bland face of Sunny Potterton smiled its chipper and highly marketable smile right at Martin. Sunny's teeth were so bright they seemed to glow between her thin, red lips. Her bobcut, blonde hair hung silky aside from the straight placed part down the center. Sunny was saying something about the alkaline levels in a good garden, and Martin was listening intently.

"Oh, God I love you, Sunny!" Martin said it aloud in his living room, loving the way her name felt as he manifested it with breath. "Sunny, Sunny, Sunny!"

Martin did love her, and to prove it to Sunny he watched her whenever she was on the talking box, and he bought all of her magazines, the home craft ones, and the wedding ones, and even the baby ones, in spite of the fact that babies gave him the willies to hell and back. Martin even bought some of the Sunny Potterton stock the moment it hit the market, and he didn't get mad when it tanked just days later.

Sunny was clean, polite, well spoken, and almost universally loved. Martin realized that he was none of these things, but he was willing to improve, and he worked hard to make his life something special.

He stood in his living room, slack-jawed, wearing a pair of blood-stained tan boxer shorts, watching Sunny Potterton plant tulips.

Martin's left eyelid began to twitch and pulse with his heartbeat, causing him to grimace. The room was quickly filling up with the chemical smell of hot metal, and Martin recoiled, taking a step back from the T.V. The talking box was starting to glow, giving Martin an instant and pounding pain in his chest. Martin thought that it might be sending out some kind of signal that would erase his heart.

The unpleasant thought passed when he heard Sunny's voice speaking to him from the television.

"Martin, do you mind if I come in?"

The thought of having Sunny Potterton over for a visit overwhelmed Martin and he felt faint, but managed to nod Yes.

The talking box began to glow even brighter, and Martin watched it give birth to Sunny Potterton. The image of the garden on the television was rendered down the middle, cleaved in half, and out of the dark static oval at the center a hand emerged, shiny with fluid. The hand was delicate and had beautiful purple finger nails. It was followed by a shoulder and a head, pushing out with great exertion, and then there was an explosive belching sound followed by a wet thud as Sunny was birthed into Martin's living room, soaking wet on his old shag carpet.

Sunny began to dry immediately, sloughing off the shiny sac that she arrived in. She vomited up a puddle of what appeared to be television static and turned to Martin.

"So good of you to have me to your house!" she said with a voice that Martin thought must be full of Christmas cheer all year round.

"So, Martin, what have you been up to?"

"Well…Sunny…"

He couldn't believe this was happening, and reached his right hand out to touch Sunny. His finger was greeted by a strong electric shock that relayed itself to his brain and extremities and nearly floored him.

"Sorry, Martin, I'm still an electronic transmission."

Martin frowned, realizing he couldn't get as close to Sunny as he wanted to without getting a nasty jolt. He wondered if an electronic transmission could bleed.

"No, I won't bleed, Martin. I can tell what you're thinking and I don't have to tell you I frown on discourtesy."

"Sorry, Sunny. Why have you come to visit me?"

"Well, Martin, I've come to help you with your spring cleaning."

Martin wondered at Sunny's perfect timing. He'd already been cleaning for days, and now he had the world's foremost cleaning expert in his own house as a special helper.

Martin thought that God must finally be rewarding him for all the hard work he'd done on his Sparkle Shrine. This electronic Sunny was his prize for years of working in the shadows, carving skin and bone and muscle, killing only those who would not be missed. The Sparkle Shrine was not yet completed, so Martin was surprised that God had responded so prematurely. Maybe this was a test…

"Okay, Sunny, you can help me with my spring cleaning, and then I'll show you what you were sent here to see."

Sunny smiled, sunshine bleach bright teeth gleaming.

"Okay, Martin, let's get to work."

Martin and digital Sunny scoured the house, soaking floors in bleach, spreading potpourri, and opening windows to let in the cool night air. Martin did most of the manual labor while Sunny gave instructions and offered advice.

"You can get rid of all that hair in the dishwasher by adding a saline solution next time you run a hot cycle."

And

"A heavy cologne, one with a real musk to it, will not only cover up the smell of the cordite but mask any traces."

And

"You know a simple flower trim would really make that vat of acid more of a centerpiece and bring a sense of light to your basement."

And

"If you shift these body parts to Tupperware and refrigerate them they'll last much longer than in your standard shoebox."

Martin was glowing, bright with his own sweat and reflecting the static shimmer of Sunny Potterton's electric skin.

After six steady hours of intensive cleaning Martin was wiped out, aching at every joint. Sunny urged him towards further work but he was fatigued beyond his limits, and believed he had proven himself. He was ready to show Sunny the Sparkle Shrine.

At his request, Sunny followed Martin up to his bedroom. Her feet singed the carpet beneath her, trailing tiny wisps of smoke.

Once upstairs, Martin led Sunny to his bedroom. He opened the door for her and walked past the large man that was tied to his bed. The man was bald, naked, soaked to the bone with sweat, and bleeding from the inside of his left eye where Martin had previously performed a home lobotomy. He was bound to the bed with piano wire sunk deep into his wrists and ankles, and his mouth was gagged with duct tape and an oven mitt. Part of the man's small intestine had been pulled through an incision in the skin of his belly, and hung wet to his left side.

The man was surrounded by arts and crafts supplies, poster boards, twine, glue sticks, stamps, pinking shears, and shiny star stickers, the same kind that Sunny used on her show. The man woke as Sunny and Martin entered the room, and passed back into unconsciousness seconds later, his eyes rolling, showing their whites.

Martin paid no attention to the man. He knelt before Sunny and asked if she wanted to see his Shrine. She sighed and said, "Yes."

Martin looked to the sky, whispered, "Please let her love it," and opened the door to the converted closet.

The black pixels at the center of Sunny's electronic eyes multiplied as her pupils dilated. She was the first witness to Martin's life's work.

Flesh was tanned and strapped around bones, bones were bound by tendons, tendons crisscrossed and were nailed into the wall with pushpins. Bowls sat in a perfect circle around the mass of tissue, each bowl containing a preserved body part. There were shriveled eyes, lips, noses, testicles, labia, fingers, ears, nipples, tongues.

Martin's favorite part of the whole thing was the glitter. He had covered everything in glitter, gold and purple and green glitter, so that it sparkled in even the faintest light. He felt his face flush with blood and pride as he turned to Sunny for approval.

Martin felt the world turn to liquid beneath his feet when he saw Sunny frowning.

Martin felt the world turn to shame as Sunny's face changed and twisted, darkened. Sunny's bronzed skin and high cheekbones had become sullen and scrunched.

"Well, Martin, I can appreciate your work ethic here. You've certainly been laboring away, and I appreciate the symmetry, but…"

Martin's heart kept sinking, deeper and deeper still.

"…but, frankly, it's sub-par work. The glitter seems, well, amateurish, and the arrangement of bits and pieces is ultimately distracting. It takes away from whatever meager power the main attraction may have had. Also, and I hope you've picked up on this too, it reeks of death. Bleach is a must, my friend."

"But, Sunny…"

"Please don't interrupt me, Martin. I've enjoyed our time together, and I hope you have too, but I've got to be going. Just one final bit of cleaning to be done…"

The look in Sunny's eyes changed. Her brow furrowed forward and shadows filled her eye sockets.

"Martin, do you know what an aberration is?"

"Nope, Sunny. Why? Do I have one? If I show you my

aberration will you stay here?"

"No, Martin. An aberration is something that must be cleansed from every surface. It is something so dirty that the world can't tolerate it."

Sunny took another carpet-singe step towards Martin.

"The weird thing about aberrations is that they're supposed to be self-destructive, but every once in a while they mutate and survive. It's very…un-tidy. So, someone else must clean them up. I'm a professional, trust me on this."

She reached out and touched Martin's chest. His heart seized up and rattled his ribcage with tight tremors. He collapsed to the floor, sending shock-spirals of glitter into the air. He couldn't move. He struggled for breath and watched Sunny clean his bedroom.

He watched, weak and helpless, as Sunny Potterton gingerly disassembled his life's work. He watched her static soaked hands systematically shatter the carefully bound bones of his Sparkle Shrine.

He watched as Sunny delicately opened the mouth of the man in his bed. She pried his jaw wide with one hand and then inserted the index finger of her right hand deep into his mouth, as if to pluck out a pimento that had lodged in his trachea. The man began to blister immediately as the electricity brought him a quick death.

Martin's chest tightened again, and he had to gulp down breath between pounding heartbeats. He hung his head and struggled to breathe as the electric Sunny destroyed all he had created.

He was shocked to find he could feel everything she was doing in his hands and body.

In the aftermath of the attack the air was thick with the cloying smell of exposed rot. Martin was curled into fetal position on the floor. He could no longer see Sunny and wondered where she had gone.

He heard a voice, familiar and somehow still comforting, calling to him.

"Martin…Martin…"

It was Sunny. She was calling to him from his living room.

He stood and stumbled towards her. He followed her burning footsteps in the carpet down the stairs and into the living room, where he saw her crouched in front of the television, one hand already immersed in its glowing surface.

"I've got to go back, Martin. I've got a rigorous schedule, and I feel my work is done here. Overall I love what you've done with the place. Maybe I'll see you again."

The black oval in the center of Martin's talking box opened wide and pulled Sunny back in, sealing off with the sound of Sunny's cold, business-like laughter.

Martin reached out to the glowing screen where Sunny was talking about the seasonal life of orchids. He wanted so badly to be in there with her, especially now that his life here had been destroyed. He watched her soft, blonde hair lilting in the autumn wind; saw her hands diving into black soil to make room for seeds. He wanted to be with her. He thought that he might be able to make Sunny bleed in that world, if he could get in. He grabbed the sides of the talking box, reared his head back, and swung it forward.

A corona of fire bloomed from the glass where his head shattered the screen. Electricity sparkled across the surface of his blackened flesh like so much glitter.

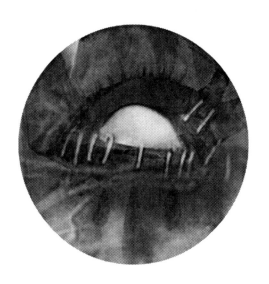

LAST THOUGHTS DRIFTING DOWN

I.mpact bears fruit. A great blossom of fire is given to the world in one billionheat moment. So fast, and full, and the sky knows what it is to be swallowed up, to be designed and undone, to give power to heat as a parasite, to fail in the face of a formula that solves itself (600 billionths of a second to make the introduction, uranium-233 a seed to bloom to tree to cloud).

And something above becomes nothing below, feathers to dust, and with the taste, that first life, the introduction to *other* creates

I

Am. and the feeling is not one of being torn apart but rather of being put together, as if all the matter before me was part of the whole and just misunderstood the potential for growth.

But I educate.

And everything that was I, and tried to run, is torn to Us, loose atoms at last, joining me, slipping back fast to the ever expanding

I

of the storm.

To be perceived is to be understood. Those that become part of I leave traces, thoughts, and though nothing slows there is a feeling of moving backwards, of understanding that I have been

Made. in the minds first. My initial vibrations created synaptic tremors, bred obsessions, turned thoughts black and spread logicancer. Hot, slick foreheads dripped sweat upon blueprints, the fluid from flesh trying to blot the ink that would undo it. But the concept was indelible.

We could make this. It could work.

Should we?

Nervous laughter, shifting in chairs. They have nightmares that go unspoken, sweatdrenched fever dreams of black birds, dripping fire, tongues expanding until skulls burst. None of it stops the vibration.

A rose blooms in the desert, child of a new Trinity. Proud fathers show photos. It is an introduction.

Should we? The world applauds with fear in its bellies. It is a strange vindication for a life's pursuit.

Photos can be doctored.

I

vibrate in the minds of millions.

We want proof.

An island washed clean by my birth. My afterbirth scars the air. The land itself becomes sacred and heavy with reminders of my birthday.

As tribute the witnesses shed what had turned black inside, scream, and their cells promise to bear no children.

The. people think I am an end, but they remain as long as I do. Last thoughts move from the electric to the sub-atomic and grow dense at my center where they collide.

I can't see, how come I can't see

Our Father who art in heaven

If I can just get underground, if I can dig then

No Wake up, wake up, wake up
    I thought I'd be holding you when this happened
He owes me twenty dollars   I love you, I love you, I lo
She never got to see my face or anything
                Shit, my hair, am I burning
    It's about time   Great, now the T.V. won't work
I can't even remember   Where's mom, oh
        Breathe, just close your eyes, and bre

Destroyer. Some think it (even those who view my birth as a blessing think it at the moment I touch them and sink white silhouettes into stone behind them).

An old man with a placard predicting my arrival yells "Destroyer, unholy light, bringer of death" before I wash through him.

He's smiling as he yells, as if I am an old friend. His last thought is thankful.

You finally came.

I deliver him to dust, and slow. The feeling throughout my body is heavy and

I

drift
down

and spin within my own winds. I move with siltskin and vomit ash from a million mouths.

Last thoughts turn to lightning in purple bruiseblack clouds. Few remain to witness my glory.

Of. those that still breathe, no lungs go untouched. Alveoli implode, hearts boil.

I

change but never stop growing.

Each cell introduced becomes part of a chain. Eyes burn, blood coughed to the ground is granted a new purpose.

To contain what I have become. To radiate and sing my secrets to anyone who passes, to spin a siren song as old as seawater and promise change.

Worlds. are within me now, the knowledge of every cell that spins to earth as ash and falls to soak the soil with my legacy.

Others exist within me, cradled in my heat, moving stones and breathing with new plastic insect faces. In concrete rooms beneath the soil there are mothers sneaking potassium iodide into baby formula and cursing now extinct world leaders. Others steal televisions that will never run again. Some stab, some rape, some run forward as if I have an end just beyond the horizon. Their skin soon knows my secrets and learns to sing, each cell vibrating in tune. A woman weeps next to a dog kennel filled with dust. A man is carried across the ground in a suit made from cockroaches. A small boy makes snow angels in the ash and smiles at the clouds.

There is an echo, a question whispered beneath my swirling winds.

Should we?

There are cities painted black, populated by blast-shadows.

From the cities, no response.

SWIMMING IN THE HOUSE OF THE SEA

The retard is finally asleep, which is great because now I can head down to the hotel swimming pool and relax. I can finish off this gut punch of a day without thinking about the blown engine on my sedan, or the lung-sucking heat tomorrow's sunshine will bring.

It's time to get this nasty, reeking desert sweat off my skin and just float in the clear, chlorinated water. I picture myself, arms and legs extended wide, a big floating X in Hawaiian print shorts. I'll close my eyes and hover there in the safe, sanitized water, floating static and alone while the world rotates around me. I can let the cool water roll into my ears and amplify the sound of my heart.

I grab my plastic key card with its generic sun-and-palm-tree logo and the words "Casa Del Mar Resort Hotel- Bakersfield, CA" across the top. I slip it into my swim shorts pocket and seal the Velcro shut. I don't grab one of our ratty, dishrag-thick room towels; there should be some plushies down by the pool.

I take a quick look at my brother, Dude, who is seventeen and still wearing pajamas with Looney Tunes on them. His too-far-apart eyes are twitching beneath his eyelids, which I read as deep sleep. The sound of his breathing fills up the room, eclipsing even the hum of the air conditioner. His thick snore is the final nail in the coffin of my evening's eligible bachelorhood. Even if I could find a girl to hook up with in this festering armpit of a city, I can't bring her back to the Snore Suite at Casa Del Mar.

I close the hotel door behind me, clipping off the sound of my retarded brother's stertoric breathing. I hate the sound of Dude's breathing, when he's asleep. It's like he has to fight the air to pull it in, all sniffles and snoring and open-mouth rasping. Or, as my dad once said to my mom, before their divorce two years ago, "Maybe Dude can't breathe right because God wants him to stop."

"Stop what?" asked Mom.

"Stop breathing, living, all of it. Maybe God's hoping he'll give up and die."

Dad was a charmer back then, right before the marriage fell from its hippie foundation. Mom decided that Jesus was her new savior, and told Dad that he had to stop making acid in the tub. Dad got turned off by Mom's newfound fire-and-brimstone, her nightly Bible readings, her orthodox self-improvement. He shuttled his drug engineering to placate her and secretly reinvested his energies in the pursuit of free love.

Free love turned out to be an ex-Hell's Angel harem member who claimed to have been in a gang-bang with Sonny Barger and Bob Dylan back in '65. Her name was Jasmine and she still lived in LaLaLand, Dad's preferred real estate.

Jasmine lets my dad drink Jack Daniels from her cooch.

Dads will tell you this kind of shit after a divorce. They think it affirms a newfound buddyhood. The illicit info just bugs me out, but I don't tell him. He seems happy, to a degree. The older I get, the harder it is for me to question the guy's decisions. He's just some older version of me that got caught up in some responsibility barbwire. My Mom's Christ fixation popped the wheel on their party bus. Dad scoped out the life ahead of him, realized living with a bum, a mongoloid, and a Bible-thumper wasn't going to cut it, and bailed. His decision to run makes sense to me, but it kills the odds on us ever being buddy-buddy.

I only have to see him once a month anyway, when I pick Dude up in L.A. and bring him back to my Mom's place in Modesto.

I run the I-5 errand for Mom, Dude's custody deal stays

smooth, and I get free rent at my Mom's townhouse in lovely northern Cali.

The free rent soothes the sting of being a twenty-one-year-old college drop-out, and it opens up a lot of bonus cash for things like clothes, weed, and new tattoos. So, to supplement my video store clerk income, I make this long, hot drive once a month.

It's retard trafficking, and I dig the kickbacks.

Casa Del Mar is a shade short of seedy. The wallpaper varies, floor-to-floor, and there's an odor hovering in the air, with the particles of carpet sanitizer. It's the smell of trapped people, desperation; it's the smell of nervous drug deals, inescapable affairs, lonely masturbation, junk-food binges that spray the air with fructose and crumbs. It's the smell that's coming from me, the stale sweat that a bad auto-breakdown in the middle of the desert has soaked me with.

I can't wait to get clean; there's just one more set of stairs till I hit the lobby floor and the swimming pool. The elevator is, of course, stationary for the time being (although a lovely computer-printed sign did apologize for the inconvenience).

I get to the pool entrance, scan my room card, unlatch the door, and walk onto the tile floor. The pool is standard hotel issue, nothing fancy, and the depth tops out at six feet, which means no diving (unless I want to surface sans teeth). There's a hot tub to my right, full of foamy bubbles. Someone must have had laundry detergent on their shorts when they went in.

There's a large, square skylight over the pool, but it's been steamed opaque by the overactive hot tub, and I can't see all the stars. Shit, the star view's got to be one of the only reasons to inhabit a Godless desert like this.

There aren't any plush hotel towels in the area, so I'll have to drip dry on the walk back to my room. Hopefully the hotel catches a little carpet mildew as a trade off for my inconvenience.

The chlorine smell to the air is pervasive, which I find comforting. Caustic chemical odors make me feel safe inside, protected from the bacterial traces of other hotel residents.

I set my key card on the tile in the far left corner of the pool area, looking over my shoulder as I do it, despite the absence of any other pool-goers. Then I jump into the deep end, feet first, and the water splashes up and feels perfect on my skin. Cool, and clean, and mildly astringent. I dip my head under and push off of the wall with my feet, shooting to the other end of the pool with a few strokes of my arms. I open my eyes just before I hit the wall, and the chlorine burns, but the view saves me from smashing headfirst into the circular light mounted at the shallow end of the pool. I close my eyes again, and stand up.

My heart is beating fast as I surface, and I feel the water rolling down my skin, sloughing off the sweat, and engine stink, and frustration of the day. I reach up to push the excess water away from my eyes with the back of my hands. I hear the door to the pool area slide open, then hard, flat shoes on tile. Then, a voice.

"All right, sport, up and out. Pool's closin'."

I open my eyes and see an eighty-year-old man wearing a hotel security outfit, the type of outfit that's vaguely cop-like, but not so derivative the guy could spend his after work hours impersonating a real officer. For example, there's a white iron-on reading "Casa Del Mar Security - Rollins" where a badge would normally be. Still the guy's got a take-no-shit demeanor to his creaky, old voice, and his shoes are so spit-shined I can see my pale face reflected in the tips. I'm confused by what the geriatric justice dealer is croaking at me so I ask him a question.

"Excuse me, Rollins..."

"Mr. Rollins, young man."

"Okay. Yeah, sorry about that. Mr. Rollins, the brochure up in my hotel room said adult swim is until eleven."

I can see the guy looking me up and down, catching the tattoos, the earrings, making quick judgments, deciding to take the zero bullshit approach.

"Brochure's wrong. Pool's till ten, hot tub's till eleven."

I'm not sure how I can respond to this, but I know that I need to swim more, that one lap hasn't shaken the dirty aura of the day off of me. I smile and shoot for polite, even though inside my head every single one of my friends is laughing at how soft I'm playing this situation.

"Okay, Mr. Rollins, I certainly understand hotel guidelines, and intend to respect them, but do you think I can swim for maybe twenty more minutes? I swear I won't drown or make a mess, and I'll be a happy hotel resident. I could be here for days, you know, my transmission blew out today and I'm pretty much stranded until my Mom FedEx's some cash."

Rollins looks like he wants to throw up on me, on my hokey obsequiousness, on my reliance on my mother. I can see inside his head.

The little puke needs money from his Mommy. When I was his age I'd already fought in the Great War and started a 400-acre dairy.

"Nope, hotel needs you out of the pool at ten. We've got automatic chlorine. Stay in past ten and you'll get burnt. Up and out."

So there I am, up and out, dripping but not ready to go back to the room; back to Dude and his loud, sickly breathing. I turn away from Mr. Rollins like a sullen thirteen-year-old, walk past him with my feet slapping wet on the tile like soggy fish, and twist the bubble-jet knob by the hot tub. I can hear his ancient voice-box rattling behind me again.

"Hot tub's only till eleven. Then it's up and out."

I don't even respond. I stare down at the mountain of foamy bubbles and wait for the old bastard to hobble on to other duties. It's a relief when I hear the door close again.

The hot tub is a poor substitute for the calm, cleansing waters of the pool. The heated water doesn't smell half as chlorinated and there's a dead wasp floating near the drainage bucket, little legs raised to the sky, like he's frozen in a permanent backstroke.

The water feels too hot; the steam from the surface is on my skin like new sweat. Unclean. Hot and unclean. Too many Goddamn bubbles; I'm waiting for a floating Lawrence Welk to pop up and play me a tune. I consider making a beard out of the bubbles, Abe Lincoln-style, but the urge passes. Mr. Rollins already infantilized me enough. I lean forward with my hands in front of me and watch the bubbles squiggle through the interstices of my fingers. It is mildly soothing, and I start to relax until I hear the pool door opening again. I'm ready to fight Mr. Rollins tooth-and-nail to stay in this rotten little tub. Maybe if I splash him he'll melt like that witch from Oz.

I crane my neck and notice with a little relief that Mr. Rollins has not returned. My new pool buddies are a couple of guys. The guy on the right is bald, with ruddy red cheeks, white chest hair, and a bit of a paunch above his black swim trunks. The guy on the left is younger, maybe my age, and has a full head of black hair, a slim moustache, a flat, nearly concave chest, and is wearing a pair of long, green surf shorts.

The young one's carrying an inflated beach ball, which seems a little off. Screw it, maybe people are really into beach balls out in Bakersfield. This is definitely the kind of town where you have to make your own fun. Earlier today I was spitting on the hot concrete beside my broken down ride, timing how long the saliva sizzled before evaporating.

I watch the new guys for a moment, to make sure they don't steal my room card. My paranoia goes into overdrive when I travel. Everyone wants to steal everything I own. I relax and remind myself that all I really have right now is my gimpy brother, some stale bagels, and a business card for the auto shop I left the sedan at earlier today. Not exactly the Ark of the Covenant, but you never know what some people will try to steal.

The two guys step into the pool, and I think about telling them about the automated chlorine, but decide not to. It could have been a deviant lie on behalf of Mr. Rollins. Besides, it might be more fun to watch these guys get a chemical burn before Rollins comes back to lay down the law.

I turn back to my tiny bubbles and try to ignore the splashing noises to my right. I massage my right leg, aching from the pedal pushing I'd done until the tranny blew out on the highway. The jets seem to have cooled the water in the hot tub down a few degrees, so I decide to put my face under the water. I want to let the water rush into my ears so that all I can hear is my heart and the movement of the water around me.

The water seems a little grimy, so I just hover there, with my face an inch from the surface of the water, running my hands through my hair. The warmth of the water and the mist from the bursting bubbles is actually pretty soothing, and pushes me towards drowsy. I snap out of that right away, and lean back against the tub wall. The idea of passing out in the tub spooks me to the marrow. What if I didn't wake up? Would the hotel staff find me in the morning, a skinny, tattooed slab of roast beef, pink flesh floating off the bone ready to carve? I picture Mr. Rollins throwing a sprig of parsley on my corpse, then gesturing to the hotel staff. "All right, he's done. Up and out."

My guts are starting to heat up and the tub doesn't feel fun anymore, but if I bail too soon I'll feel like Mr. Rollins has won. Won what?

I start to look for an answer in my head but I'm distracted by the sound of my new pool buddies batting the beach ball back and forth. They're laughing and saying things to each other, but the weird tile acoustics in here muffle everything. They seem happy.

I wonder if Dude would like to play a game like that? Simple fucker, I'm sure he would. I could wake him up, bring him down here and introduce him. The beach ball guys would laugh when I introduced my brother as Dude, myself as Wolf. People always laugh at our names. I don't bother to explain the situation to them, how our parents spent the seventies on some tripped out Kahlil/Prophet shit and decided, in all their addled wisdom, to let us name ourselves. If I ever bother to breed, I'm naming the kid before it even pops out the womb. Some nice, Biblical name. I'm sure Mom could help me come up with something.

The paunchy older guy gives the beach ball a good whack and sends it flying above the pool, a high arc of rotating color, blue, to white, to yellow, to white, to red, to white, to green, and it lands outside of the pool, rolling towards me. The heat of the tub and the noise from the Gidget brothers has killed any chance I had at relaxation, and as the ball gets closer to me I swear I'll pop it if I get the chance.

The twentysomething kid with the scrappy little moustache jumps out of the pool and picks up the ball before it has a chance to reach me. He regards me quickly, as he grabs the ball, and I give him a hard look, the good old aimless ice grill.

Aggression without reason is a bit of a stress reliever in itself. Let somebody else absorb the shit I've been through today.

The kid nearly runs back to the pool, and jumps in with a splash. I'm sure Mr. Rollins would consider that horseplay. I wish there was a convenience phone right by the hot tub so I could rat these guys out and simmer in peace.

I sink my shoulders beneath the water. I sink my head so that my eye-line is just above the tile border of the hot tub and watch Paunchy and the Moustache Kid play their mutant beach ball game. There are no apparent rules, they're just batting the thing back and forth, but the Moustache Kid asserts he is winning. He screams it up at the skylight. "I'm winning! I'm winning!"

Watching them play makes me think about Dude, about how we used to kick a soccer ball back and forth for hours in the back yard while Mom and Dad sat on the porch and roasted J's and listened to Iron Butterfly. Special times, right? Didn't last though, because I kept growing and Dude didn't, really. By the time I hit high school Dude had left standard issue brother status behind and become My Retarded Brother. Our parent's marriage was beginning to crack around the acid-fried edges, and a lot of the responsibility for Dude got sent my way.

I dodged it, begged out, and abandoned the duty. I figured I'd only be young once, what right did my parents have to saddle me with their mutant chromosomes. I hadn't even really talked to Dude for two years, when Mom offered me the free rent/mongoloid transport trade off.

We still don't talk much, although Dude likes the sound of his own voice, and will go on at length about cartoons, and sailboats, and his beloved Elton John. When he gets agitated on car rides, we listen to Elton John's "Carla Etude" over and over again, till he chills out.

I hate Elton John. I hate "Carla Etude." I hate bad transmissions and overpriced mechanics and crying brothers that can't be reasoned with because the Elton John tape is stuck in the deck of my broke-ass sedan. I hate all these movies that make retards look like saints and idiot savants, because I spend a lot of time with Dude, and all he seems like to me is a fucking broke-ass person whose brain won't click over and work. Yeah, I sort of hate Dude.

I hate these guys to my right, playing baby games in the pool I was supposed to be relaxing in.

I keep watching them and now they're wrestling with each other, and I wonder if this place is turning into a Roman bath house. They're smiling, and laughing, and pulling each other's hair. The Moustache Kid leaves long scratch marks on Paunchy's back.

I couldn't see it before, but I do now. I thought they might be business men ending a long day of conferences, or some kind of daffy foreign sports enthusiasts.

No, these guys are together.

This beach ball business is foreplay. Some kind of weird, childish foreplay killing my last shot at chilling out.

My dogshit day has fully invested itself in me. I'm seething, angry in my bones.

I have to do something.

I pop out of the hot tub, jump into the pool, and snatch the multi-colored beach ball from the Moustache Kid's hands before he can even comprehend what's going on. Then, as quickly as I got in, I'm out, dripping on the tile with their ball clutched under my left arm. I turn to face the guys.

The Moustache Kid looks five seconds from crying, and it's a weird, questioning look on his face that I can't fathom, so I turn to Paunchy and say, "Pool time's over. Up and out."

I pop their beach ball in between my hands, and feel the stale air move across my wet skin. Paunchy is coming towards me, his face and bald scalp bright red.

I hit the light switch and bail out of the pool entrance, leaving the buddies back in blackness. I begin to run, wanting to enjoy this but not quite able to bring any laughter to the surface.

I hear the pool entrance open behind me, then slam shut. I run a little faster as heavy, bounding footsteps rush up behind me.

Before I can react, there are wide, heavy hands upon my shoulders, spinning me around a like a little top and grabbing me firm again. Then I'm being slammed into the wall behind me, and I'm face to face with Paunchy, feeling cheap plaster tinkling down on my scalp where my head impacted the wall.

Paunchy's breath is on my face, hot, and he's got me looking right into his wide, brown eyes.

"Why?" he asks.

"Why what?" I play dumb. Paunchy won't stand for it and gives me another good smack into the wall.

"Why? Why do people like you have to ruin everything?"

"Ruin what? Your stupid little game, your faggy little pool party?" I'm about to piss myself, but Paunchy's reaction is so unexpected that part of me is still tweeking, playing tough. And I don't know where the "faggy" business comes from. The whole straight/gay thing is a non-issue to me. Pick a hole, have at it. I don't care.

Paunchy shakes me again, demanding my attention, his eyes on the verge of tears.

"You think we're gay? What do you know? You don't know anything; people like you just want to take things away, to hurt people like me, like my son. My son is crying now, back in that pool, and I've left him alone."

I'm nervous, beginning to stammer, confused. "Yeah, but the guy should be able to handle himself, he's like twenty…"

"You fucking jerk, my son is schizophrenic. He can't handle things like a normal twenty-year old. That's why he's crying right now. Because of you. The kid never has fun, his brain's got him all twisted up, and he's scared all the time, like he's stuck in hell. But he was smiling tonight, he liked the game, he liked the pool, and you took that away. And for what? I mean, can you tell me why?"

I have no answer for the man. Which is bad, because he's balling one of his fists and I'm thinking he might want to beat an answer out of me. Where's Mr. Rollins when I'm about to be maimed?

Paunchy shakes me again, just short of furious.

"Why did you have to mess with us?"

I have no answer for the man.

His son exits the pool and approaches us, stops just short of my right shoulder. His eyes are red and bleary. He speaks. "Hey, Dad?"

Paunchy takes a deep breath, then responds, "Yes, Michael?"

"Dad, there aren't any towels by the pool."

"Well, there should be some back at the room. Do you know where that is?"

"Yeah, Dad."

"Okay, well, head on up and I'll meet you in a sec', okay?"

"Okay." The Moustache Kid walks away and turns to the stairwell. He is shivering, although the hotel is stifling hot.

The kid is shivering because of me, because I popped his ball and left him behind, in the dark. His dad leans in close to my face, our lips almost touching, his eyes deadlocked to mine.

"I'm going to go take care of my son."

I want to say sorry, to say something, but nothing comes across my lips.

Paunchy throws his meaty right fist into my soft belly and I hit the floor. He spits a quick, harsh "Fuck you" before turning to the stairwell.

I manage to retain my lunch and start breathing again. I half walk, half crawl my way up the stairs to my floor.

I reach into my Velcro shorts pocket and come up with nada. My Casa Del Mar room key is still down at the locked pool, but I don't want to risk running across Mr. Rollins, or head to the front desk and ask for a replacement.

I knock on the door for two minutes before Dude wakes and opens it. He's confused, and tired, and wants to know why I'm bleeding.

I tell him I took a bad dive, down at the pool, that the deep end wasn't deep enough. I don't mention the large, angry man who decided to crack some drywall with my skull.

Dude walks me over to our bathroom, the legs of his rayon pajamas whisping against each other. I sit down on the toilet and Dude puts a towel to my head, which has developed a steady, jackhammer throb. Dude presses the towel down too hard, while he's trying to staunch the blood seeping from my split scalp. It hurts, sending quick, white-fire pain down my spine, and I lash out with my left arm, pushing Dude into the bathroom counter.

"Stay away from me, you fucking retard." He's out the door quick, and I flop off the toilet, then re-position myself to vomit.

I take off my clothes and crawl into the shower. I start the water up, sharp and cold, to try and wash away the whole day, the whole evening, everything. I can hear Dude crying in the other room. I'm good at that, I guess. I try, but I can't work up any crocodile tears for myself.

The shower isn't helping. I'm trying to make things right inside my head, trying to replay the pool situation in a way that doesn't make me feel like a total asshole. The cold water isn't helping my noxious headache.

I get out of the shower and dry off. I throw on some flannel pants and wrap the last clean, ratty towel around my head, and hope my scalp wound will clot soon.

I walk out to the air-conditioned hotel room and see that Dude has cried himself to sleep in his twin bed on the left side of the room. I sit on the edge of my bed and look at my brother.

My vision is blurring, and I probably have a concussion, but it feels right to look at him like this, like for once I'm the vigilant and caring older brother. I think for a moment about all the times I've told My Poor Retarded Brother stories, playing the pity card to get into some drunk girl's pants. I think about the times I've seriously considered abandoning Dude at some rest stop along the highway, picturing the guilty relief that would spread across my parent's faces when I tell them Dude had disappeared.

For the first time, the thoughts feel like poison in my bruised belly. I don't know how to shake the feeling. The digital clock on the bed stand reads 3:23. I collapse into my bed.

I can't sleep. Things are too wrong to sleep.

So, at 3:27 I slip out of my bed and into Dude's. I let one of my arms flop onto his thin chest. He wakes for a moment; his thick, unsteady breathing smoothes out. He turns his head towards me, and opens his eyes, surprised that I'm there.

"Wolf?"

"Yeah, Dude, it's me."

"Okay. Are you going to sleep by me?"

"Yeah, Dude."

"Okay. Hey, Wolf?"

"*Yeah*, Dude." The irritation I'm trying to shake comes back into my voice.

"Sorry I hurt your head earlier, Wolf. I didn't mean to."

I'm thinking, "It's okay, I know you didn't mean to, and I'm sorry I hit you, I'm sorry for so many things." I can't get the words out of my mouth. Looking at Dude's wide eyes, hearing the care in his voice, I'm almost paralyzed.

Then my whole body is shaking, and I can tell I'm a moment away from sobbing. I wrap my arms tight around Dude, and shake against my will. I don't cry out loud, because I don't want to upset him anymore. I hold the tears in and feel heat radiating from my face.

He can tell I'm upset and he runs his fingers through my hair for a moment, each finger tracing a soft line across the side of my head. Dude whispers to me.

"I know, Wolf. I know it hurts. But you're going to be okay."

It's like the little fucker wants me to cry. So I do, I break, and I cry for longer than I ever have before, and Dude just keeps running his fingers through my hair until I stop shaking.

When I'm done, all I can think to say is, "Thanks, bro."

Dude repeats it back to me. "Thanks, bro."

Those are the last words we speak before Dude slips back into sleep. I want to pass out, but I consider my probable concussion and fight to stay awake, while my brother fights to breathe.

Should he stop breathing, I'd be there to save him.

This is the oath that I swear into the too-bright sunrise, as the desert heat returns, and our hotel room at the Casa del Mar fills with new light.

WALL OF SOUND:

A MOVEMENT IN THREE PARTS

Entrance

Right at the fucking kick-off, I've got to ask you to do something you're not going to want to do.

I've got one issue before we go any further.

It's that friend you've brought with you; the friend who always carries you through darker times like this; the one who helps you wake up in the morning; the one that feeds you breakfast and better aspirations; the one that makes tomorrow seems like a birthday cake filled with cash.

Yeah, *that* friend.

You're going to have to kill him.

End him.

Push him to the ground and crack his mouth wide open; slide his teeth onto the curb until you hear enamel chipping against Reddi-Mix pavement. Start stomping.

Kill your friend. It's for your own good.

If somebody like *that* ever stepped foot in here, *in a place like this*, they'd chew a fucking hole through *you* to escape. He takes one step over this threshold, you won't survive.

I'm not the bad guy here. I'm a realist. And I'm asking you to do me a favor.

Just one favor, and we can proceed…

I. BURN/LIQUIDATION

"E-bomb?"

"Yeah, right here, yo," drops out of my mouth in response, even though I promised just about everybody I know I would go straight for a while, and even though my serotonin levels are so dangerously low I'm too depressed to even bother to kill myself, and even though, and this strikes me as particularly fucked, the kid dealing looks a lot like the old bearded Christ, and smells of cold beef and paint thinner.

The stinky guy scopes over his shoulders, digs the scene. Digs on me, a very long, sly look. He's not gay, he's just clockin' to make sure I'm not El Narco Federali. He checks out my gigantic denims, checks out the tattoos, the sunken eyes, sunken chest, sunken general demeanor, makes his assessment.

"What you need, dog?" rolls out of his mouth, low and greasy sounding over his thin, chewed on lips. Damn! Breath like hot paint thinner on this guy. Flash second passes, I wonder if he's dealing to support a hardcore paint huffer habit, but then I check myself and acknowledge that those types are so low rent they could never get up the capital to start dealing. Spend half their fucking time with "Gold Glitter" Dacryl spray paint flecked on their mugs, vomit in their hair. You get near them and you can smell the burning brain cells and almost hear the sizzle in the cerebellum, the screams of the million vanquished bits of grey matter. Huffing is like a fucking Personal Mental Genocide Program. Is that a band name? Probably. I bet...

BUY THE PILLS AND TAKE THEM!

I've got a vicious mental drift problem, so I have to force myself to focus and achieve things. Get the drug, the drug is what matters here. The e-bomb, MDMA, ecstasy. Definitely more important. Get, acquire, consume, start the party, put the jumper cables to the old kicker for one more stretch of beats and dancing. Dig on the lasers. Stinky Christ is getting impatient with my spacey behavior, so I ask, "Got any Mitsubishis of Applejacks?" Dependable old favorites.

"Nah man, nah, you don't want that shit, that shit is old, *old* old, played out," he says, slow, with emphasis on the fact that my favorite drugs are now "old old" which I guess is about as old as shit can get these days. "Nah, for twenty-five I can get you these double stack Karaoke e-bombs, or you can try the new shit."

My first reflection is this- Do I want to play guinea pig for some backwoods chemist?

Second reflection- Is this bitch looking doper just trying to pass his bunk goods off on me so he can give his quality pills to his regular customers?

Third- Is looking like Jesus a real aesthetic choice, or just something that happens to skinny white kids that don't take care of themselves, hygiene-wise?

Fourth- Why am I talking to this flipped out Christ cat when the party is really starting to go off. Especially when I could be right up by the main speakers catching some basswaves and putting some moves on that blonde doll with the pink hair and translucent angel wings?

Final reflection- None. Thoughtless. Urgency and impulse

kick in, thought replaced by need for the pill, the pleasure, and now, now, now, NOW, *NOW!*

"Yeah, lemme see the new stuff, yo." As Stinky Christ pulls his little knit (from hemp, I'm positive) satchel out from under his natty jacket I wonder when I started talking this stupid. Ending sentences with "yo" cannot sound good or reflect on me positively, in any way. Not even in a smirking, ironic, Dennis-Miller-type-asshole kind of way. I have to squat to get to my secret pocket hidden on the inner, upper right leg of my big-ass pants.

I pull out a little wad of cash, a couple of twenties and eight one dollar bills, which I will spend later on bottles of water to be consumed almost perpetually throughout the night. I have "The Dehydration" brand of drug fear, ecstasy and coke specific. The quantity and frantic quality of my e-bomb generated dance moves causes me to sweat in profusion, and I'm not sure of all the details, but I heard some shit once about liver necrosis and electrolyte washout that sounded crazy ill. Of course, on the flipside I heard about the roller who drank so much fucking water he got hydrotoxification, and died from drinking *too much* water. I only bring in eight bucks, so that I drink a lot, but don't drink so much that my body bloats like a loofah.

I unroll the twenties, make a final scope for John Law or those steroid sucking pricks that run security for these parties, and make my purchase. In the Unkempt Dealer's hand, forty bucks. In mine, two clear gel caps filled with an unknown yellow and black powder.

Quick thought. "Yo, what's in these, dog?"

The skinny kid is all smile, more of an Aum Shinrikyo smile than a Loving Savior smile. "You're gonna dig it. Some pure MDMA, some DMT, and little bit of mutant type-A streptococcus. I call 'em Roman Candles. They light you up and blow you the fuck out, yo. Peace. If you like 'em, tell your friends. I'm the ice cream man."

Funny guy, stepping up to me with that copped "yo" shit, and he has the nerve to tell me he put bacteria in my drugs. HA HA HA, that's one class act sense of humor you've got there you fucking jerk.

Laugh it up. Back in the day I would have rolled him, but now I have to kick all this peace, love, unity, and respect shit, so I walk away, towards the beats and the girls. I'm thinking, for some reason, "I'm a bigger dumb-ass than that guy."

Backlash for the violent thoughts. I've done too many drugs to play tough any more. Spell it, B-U-R-N-O-U-T. No one constant emotion, no steady thoughts.

Kicking out the rave style stroll now, part dance/part walk. Big bounce in my step, head nodding with the four on the floor basswaves being dropped by DJ Northern Light. The music is percussive, tight and jazzy. Standard bass, snare, and cymbal House arrangement, with some nice distorted bass arpeggios under it, and every third measure there's a fat keyboard stab. I'm feeling it, locked into the beat and I'm not even rolling yet. Best to play cool early, bust out a couple of dance moves, but don't get wicked. I have to save that for when everybody is high, because, ugly truth be told, I'm not the tightest dancer and I know my moves will better represent to those who are deeply and chemically fucked. If you get high enough you can watch a guy wearing a Winnie the Pooh backpack slowly spinning some glow sticks on strings, and actually think, "WOW! I am genuinely amazed at this display of talent! Hooray for this!" Which, I'm sober enough to recognize right now, is fucking ridiculous.

I go up by the speakers and scope out the party. Buzzed, majorly buzzed now, just off the music, and maybe the presence of so many girls who I know will never ask me for commitment. The right kinds of girls treat me like a party favor. They use me, then the party's over, lights go up, the drugs wear off, and I'm discarded along with the no longer glowing plastic tubes, unwanted flyers, empty water bottles, and countless wads of bubble gum.

Which is fine by me. I don't really need them as long as I've got the drugs.

JESUS H., MAN. YOU ARE A FUCKING BURNOUT! Listen to yourself.

Yeah, I better reprioritize soon, but I have parties laid out for at least the next three months. I'll get on that priority shit later, yo.

No worries. No unnecessary judgment of self. Every once in awhile my conscience likes to kick thoughts up without asking me to think them first. Like Jiminy Cricket with no Goddamn tact.

"I fucking hate myself," I'm thinking, and suddenly, too suddenly. If I'm not bi-polar, I'm working on it. I try to ignore the thought, feel the music, close my eyes and move. The place is too hot, the venue sucks, and although I like DJ Northern Light I'm not vibing off the House any more. I want some Speed Garage, some Jungle, even some Happy Hardcore, anything that will push me harder, push out the thought, make me just feel.

Time to hit up the Roman Candles.

I'm hating this party so bad I decide to give myself a good, brutal brainfuck, and I slip *both* of the pills into my hand. They sit there in the soft, lazy flesh of my hand, and they feel warm. The lasers above my head reflect dimly off the smooth gelcaps. I get a big, fat smile, and I'm thinking (or maybe just feeling), "Yeah, here we go!"

As I lift the pills to my mouth I hesitate for one tiny moment as I feel both of the e-bombs shift unexpectedly in my hand, like Mexican jumping beans. "Come on dumbfuck, there are no insects in your pills. Goddamn burnout! Eat 'em!"

Down the tubes, and it feels like they shift inside my throat too. I shouldn't
have dry swallowed. Secondary gag reflex, then it passes.

Downtime. I'm waiting for the pills to kick. I've had DMT before and I'm starting to hope there's not too much in these Roman Candles, but done is done. I saw a guy on the T.V. once who could purposefully regurgitate any item he swallowed, be it car keys, marbles, whole eggs, prophylactics, whatever. I do not possess this skill, so the pills will remain in my belly. Swimming in the nervous acid.

I'm really starting to sketch on the DMT, hoping I won't see God, or cherubim, or anything too otherworldly. People that see that type of shit have a tendency to forget to breathe. I'm a lifetime respirator. Breathing is my lifelong friend. Got to keep breathing. Breathing is life. I love feeling my lungs expand, sucking in the air.

Shit, now I'm thinking on it too much; I've become too self

aware of my breathing. I have to mentally contract my diaphragm. I have to will each breath. In and out, in and out, try and circular breathe, in through the nose, hold three seconds, out through the mouth. In three, hold three, out three, the magic three. Focused. Relaxing. Let the autonomic system take over, you dumb bastard.

The percussive waves pushing through the room speed up, gaining the steady stomp of sixteenths. Nice. The DJ just segued into some Hardcore. Yeah, I'm feeling this. I start walking around, spying the mean-ass grimaces on the people's collective faces, diggin' it big time. Hands in the air, frantic limbs twisting, heads really bopping, sweat dripping, some peoples eyes closing, just really *feeling it*. My nervousness assuages a little, mellows out, although I briefly get the *What If This Hallucinogen Makes Me Claw My Fucking Eyes Out Because I Think I Can Never Come Down* fear.

It is a valid fear; I've seen the fallout of a bad trip before.

Two years ago, at a house party in Modesto, I saw a girl trip so hard on her own mug in the mirror that she flipped permanent-style. She'd been staring at her face for too long, maybe five minutes, and then she started brushing her teeth with someone's old, blue toothbrush, the kind with the little red rubber thing at the end that looks like a perfect chocolate chip. She murmured something about circles, and something else about her never being clean again, none of us ever being clean, and then she started scrubbing her teeth. No water in-volved in this, just a big glob of Aquafresh Whitening and that old plastic hygiene utensil. The look on her face was so intense I had to bail, even though the bathroom was the one quiet place in the party where a kid could really just bug out on shit. Anyway, a few minutes later I'm out on the back porch, seeing purple eyeballs in the sky and all that, and I hear a girl inside screaming these awful, wet screams. Typically good blotter renders me mad coward, but I charged into the house anyway.

Mistake. In the living room, backed into the corner, was my toothbrush girl. The front of her white tank top was covered in red and white, blood and toothpaste foam. Her right hand was wrapped like a claw around the brush and it looked like the plastic bristles had been flattened. Her fingers, the utensil, and her face were all soaking crimson. Her mouth looked like a big black hole, oozing blood over her lower lip and down her neck, where some of it had already coagulated, thick like jelly, in the hollow of her throat. She looked like a trapped animal, deeply sad, deeply scared, and most of all confused.

She looked around the room, and then she dropped the toothbrush. Backed against the corner, she sunk to the floor, slow, face oozing bubbly red paste. My brain and my stomach flipped, and I darted outside, knowing that nothing good was going to happen in that room. Out on the deck I heard her start to sob, and sort of scream at the same time. "Mommy, mommy, uagghh, I, I, I'm cleeeeeaaaann now! Clean!"

I vomited on the way to my car, smelled Chicken Noodle Soup, spilled beer, copper pennies and bile. I was too high to drive, but way, way too high to be anywhere near that nightmare. Too much ill shit. Too much reality. Too much of a fucking After School Special "Tragic Moment of the Week." I hope I never bug like that, but they don't call DMT "The Rocketship" due to its lack of effectiveness, so I have to focus, remember that nobody trips forever, except for schizos and Italian film directors.

"So," I think to myself, "what's the agenda, old sport, old chum, pally of mine?" I can't answer myself, figuring that it is kind of too late to do any planning, knowing that I just have to go along with the ride, check the vibe, maybe dance a little later, when the bomb really hits. Maybe, a couple of hours after that, find a girl, whatever, just to talk, maybe a little more. Maybe find some "buddies" doing coke. It's amazing how fast I can become close friends with somebody I spy chopping out some fat, white rails. The duration of the friendship usually lasts from the moment I find out they have coke, to the moment I start tasting that nasty, acetone-type drip. Then I run away. I actually run sometimes. Fucking tweeker. I simply cannot be trusted.

I decide to just kick around the party some more, purchase some water, enough to keep me hydrated for at least an hour. I hang on for an extra second at the bar, hoping to catch a little lingering eye contact with the hottie in the silk looking haltertop with the Japanese/ Chinese/Taiwanese/Pekinese/etc. symbol on it. She's too busy, no go. Fuck it, just keep moving. Pondering the current club kid fetish with all things Eastern, wondering how many kids out there are tattooed and variously adorned with Asian symbols that don't mean what the kids think they mean. Like my friend Perry, the dumbfuck gets a huge, black and green tattoo of a Japanese kanji symbol between his shoulder blades. Guy at the shop told him it means "courage." Two weeks later an exchange student from Daihatsu or wherever spies Perry by the Olympic size pool at the university, asks him why he has the word "eggplant" tattooed on his back. Perry was crazy pissed. Too ashamed to do anything about it, though. He trusted the lousy biker fuck at the shop, and now, barring any highly expensive laser surgery, he will spend the rest of his life proudly festooned with the word EGGPLANT, in bold ink, on flesh.

      I decide it's time to dig on some Jungle, and at thinking this I suddenly get this deep, blood level urge to hear some hard, dark, rapid beats. I really need it. The power of self-suggestion renders me frantic.

      I see kids headed down a narrow staircase towards, I hope and pray, some sort of Jungle DJ room. Shit, I didn't even check the flyer. I never do anymore. What if there's no fucking Jungle, just a bunch of Goddamn sissy ass disco-fuck booty fucking House? Fucking useless, prancy worthless disco redux bullshit!

      Whoa! Whoa there boy! Just feeling the speed of my drugs kicking in. Check pulse, verify it as way above average. Need some beats to match it. Jungle definitely, maybe even some Breakbeat. Need audio saturation, waves upon waves, the old Phil Spector Wall of Sound.

      I push my old Vans down the staircase, stepping around two fucking e-tards who clearly took their pills way too early and will probably be lying dazed and sedate in each others arms by three in the morning. The two are making out crazy fierce, sweat pouring down both of them, hips smashed together, tongues playing. Just for a moment I start to jones, then I remember, "I'm here for the music, for the party." Still, it looks like a real thrill ride. I probably wouldn't have the easiest time playing pick-up with all this DMT that's supposedly in my system, anyway. Waiting for it to hit, tick...tock...I want to be interstellar high in the next twenty minutes, I'm ready. I hit the bottom floor.

"This DJ is really punishing, man!" says the candy kid at the base of the stairs. I can't focus, the room is too hot, way too dank, and I'm sure that with each breath I'm sucking down a couple of liters of other people's vaporized sweat. These beats are so distorted, I can't even figure out what's spinning. Shit, the walls are tight, no room to dance. I'll probably pass out if I spend one more moment in here.

Fuck it, I'm heading back up topside. Out of this moist little cavity, this bacterial barn filled with kids too high to notice just how *nasty* it is in here. I pass the e-tard couple on the way back up. Christ, it looks like a conjugal visit. As I roll by I say, "Yo, the Olympic Dry Humping Team try-outs are next week. Damn!" It sounded kind of clever in the split second where I generated the thought and decided to speak it, but as it's coming out of my mouth I can't help feeling oafish, gawky, and weird. I guess I get kind of bitchy when I'm waiting for pills to kick.

I head back into the main room, which is now definitely where it is at. The kid up top is still spinning Hardcore, some real rough, *You Are All Going To Be Killed By Giant Robots Owned By Multi-National Corporations* kind of Hardcore, with distortion that is just ripping my face off. I scope around, see kids sitting down already. Probably whacked some Ketamine, forgot how to move. Dumb.

I'm trying to dance, starting to hop a little bit, getting the arms into it, putting on a big smile. Problem is, the Hardcore, combined with the rising sensation of being vaguely high is just making me mean. I feel like throwing up a fist or something, some kind of Slayer concert aggression. Knowing that any particular type of testosterone induced behavior would be frowned upon amidst this neutered "New Disco" set, I chill and head up towards the front to watch the DJ. Maybe he's really cutting it up.

Here at the front of the room the DJ is oblivious to his audience. He seems to be concentrating on one knob on the mixer in particular, although with each of his manipulations I hear no actual change in the track. Wanker DJ style, making dramatic motions for the crowd while in actuality afraid to really mess with the mix, and make the song his own. Timid DJ's deserve no credit. The records are spinning fast, the BPM on the mixer looks outrageous, and it looks like one of the records is by an artist called "Darkstep" which for some reason puts a feeling of terror in my belly. I realize I have about five seconds before my Rocketship takes off, the vibe is rising like electric waves. My nerves are acid tight and I can feel a strange burn just under the skin, like you get from eating too much niacin before a tox screen.

Finally, here we are. Highsville, USA.

Population: Me.

Mad pressure behind my eyes, like my systolic and diastolic just found out they were going to have an unwanted baby. I hope my blood pressure isn't swelling the veins on my neck and forehead because it makes me look like the fucking devil, and I'm still thinking of getting my mack on, or at least finding a girl to get a back rub from, if I get too bugged out. Tingling on my scalp, like that "egg crack" thing kids used to do on top of each others heads back in second grade.

For one moment everything in my peripheral stops moving, like painted walls close on each side of me, and then, a moment later everything moves into top speed, playing catch up. Big grin from me, face spread tight, too happy, almost like a rictus, a grimace. Unnatural happy, like I can't shake it. Fuck it, even a overbearingly dumb grin is better than the typical hallucinogen addled expression a.k.a. The Zoned Out Space Case Look. The empty "I just whacked back a brick of dusted cat tranquilizer and now I don't know where I am, who I am, or how to move/ Dawn of the Dead" type look.

I don't ever want to rock that style, and shit, now I'm thinking about zombies, ashen faces, bloody toothbrushes, etc. Which is bad under normal circumstances and tragic on DMT so I rush over to a speaker bank to try and clean my brain out. The good old Sonic

Chimney Sweep.

Concentrate on the beats, focus, hear the layers, don't think in circles. I grab the speaker grill right in front of one of the bass reflex areas, feel the waves, the warm air expelled across my forehead feels perfect, like a light breeze on a sunny day. I close my eyes and there's swirling sunshine trapped beneath the lids, shifting, bright, with little purple and green bubbles in it. YES. The breeze from the speaker is giving me full body tingles, every inch is pulled tight, every tiny little hair on my head, my arms, the back of my neck is feeling the basslines, and I want to throw my head back in some sort of exaltation, but I fear that any tiny movement will alter the body high.

How long can I stand here like this, mated to the goddamn speaker? How long before some coked out little candy raver tries to give me some Vicks? How long before I get bumped into? How long until some concerned little rave citizen asks me if I'm okay, do I need some water, or some gum, or something? Which of course I don't need, and yes I'm perfectly okay, unbelievably okay right here in my little e-tard womb, as long as nobody messes with me.

I am content, and I imagine that this is what people who achieve Zen feel like, and then realize that if it is, I've really cheated my way into it. Forty dollars for perfect Zen, what a great fucking deal! Wait, I can feel eyes on me now. Bad eyes watching. What? Oh, don't let me get the Fear, I'm like praying to whoever is up there and presides over tripped out little guys who get in too deep. Refocus, catch the music again, trap it inside my head. New agenda: MOVE!

I can't.

Which is bad.

Which is so very fucking *deeply bad.*

Um, oh shit, oh shit, oh shit. Move, move move move move move!

This feels wrong. My eyes won't open. I know my heart is beating, I can feel it in my neck, along the carotid and jugular, and I must be breathing, although I can't feel much shift in my chest.

MOVE! My body is not receiving commands. Fucking synapses aren't connecting or something.

A new body high hits me. Right up my spine, sharp. Strychnine? No, not an option, don't overthink, don't panic. *MOVE!* A new skin tingle, like tacks being shot into me, then melting away. Not definitely painful, but bad. Maybe. *PLEASE MOVE!* Shit, this is hazy. I keep fading my thoughts out. Just as I almost have one, really grasp it and think it, it blasts away with my pulse. *PLEASE JUST MOVE! ANYTHING! DON'T FREEZE LIKE THIS!*

Across my arms I feel these alien tickles, like insect motion, and I can't brush it away. Then it whips through my arms, up the front of my chest (am I breathing?) and surges up behind my eyelids, pregnant with unwanted visions. In front of my eyes there is some kind of tapestry, real seventies style, lots of pastels, paisley, some ornate horse drawings. Yes, definitely horses, with dark black scales. Fucking...what... lizard horses? *MOVE!* This is not good. I don't like this. I can't control this. The lizard horses start to run, black scales dropping off their rib cages, exposing dark blue liquid innards. They are charging away from me, hooves kicking up purple spots that rotate and smash into each other as they speed by my head, wherever *that* is. *JUST FUCKING MOVE NOW!* Just a toe, or an eyelid, or my feet or something. Maybe I'm okay. No. Can't remain inactive. Why can't I hear anything? Where did the music go?

Then ....BAM!............. and the music screams back into my head, my eyes pop open. OhthankGod! Eyes under control, move something else. I shift my head up slowly, it feels dense, and there's more pressure behind my eyes, like weights stitched to the optic nerve, seeking the ground. I want to get to the restroom, throw some water on my face, maybe sit down further away from the music. Oh shit, my hands burn. I must have been smashing them into the speaker grates. I peep at them, and know I must be out-of-my-noggin fried, because it looks like they are bleeding, like the speaker grates sunk right into them, the criss-cross pattern pushed into my skin. I recall the sage old Geto Boys, realize my mind must be playing tricks on me. It really looks likes I'm bleeding though. Fuck it, even if it is real I'll just suffer the wound, and remember not to press against the grate so hard next time. I head towards the restroom. Everyone I walk past seems made of plastic, even though they are moving. Like little machines, each engineered for one specific task. Look, there's the machine that hops up and down, and over there is the little thing that just nods its head, and there's the good old "passed out in a puddle of his own vomit" machine, and to my left is the "chewing holes through her own cheeks because she forgot the fucking bubblegum and is clearly remiss about it, and doesn't know quite what to do" machine, and by the wall we have the "stretching-its-calves" machine, number 112558.

My little world, everyone else is plastic.

Shove my hands in my pocket, and they really do hurt, sharply. Damn. I'm probably bleeding all over my sixty dollar denims. As I walk away the DJ looks sinister, hunched over the decks like he has some kind of weapon inside and he is just waiting for the perfect time to unleash it. Diabolical DJ and his Sinister Set.

I have taken some very bad pills, and I would now like some help, some comfort, some anything but this. I've got it bad now, The Fear, but I've had it before, and I can ride it out.

How? I'm surrounded by machines. Bits of plastic, minds of silicon/carbon composite. The floor feels like it is yielding too much. Quicksand? Mind explosion. Picturing: slow death, no one reaching in to help me out, water and sand down my gullet, in my eyes. Out think this, damn it! Get to the bathroom.

I finally get to the restroom door, or rather it rushes up to meet me after a few confused and nauseous moments of staggering, and as I head in I remember one of my rules, which is to never go near mirrors while tripping. Monsters in there, monsters in me. I flush water into my face, turn away from the mirror and dig on two shirtless guys, absolutely glitter-soaked, licking each other's hands. E-tard shit is almost enough to make me smile, but something seems desperate about their passion, empty, and besides, I've suddenly realized I need to piss.

I push past the licking buddies and into the bowels of the restroom, which is, of course, already flooding, and reeks of vomit.

Focus, unbutton my pants. Say howdy to the unit, give it the ol' wink like " 'Ello there chap." I can feel pressure in my bladder, but the urine won't flow. Staring at the wall in front of me, I spy a fucking old, green booger somebody was clever enough to smear there. There is a thick black nostril hair caked into it, with a crusty white follicle hanging pendulously at its end. My eyes can feel the weight at the base of the follicle, the slight urgings of gravity versus the co-efficient of friction that holds the follicle and hair firmly to the snot. I'm seeing in too much detail. The wall suddenly seems forty feet away; the trip is distorting my depth perception. I don't want to force a piss, but there will be people waiting behind me soon, and the muffled sound of the beats is somehow scary in this florescent lit little hole. I look down at my dick again, try and visualize myself urinating. Like coach said, "Picture it inside your head and then make it happen." There we go. It's warm, too warm and sort of burning. More bad, just more and more bad from these pills.

"If I fucking find that dealer..." I think, but the pain at the head of my unit stops me from even thinking. I look down and see that the tail end of my stream of urine is rose colored. Shit. Blood from my hands? No. More and more bad, and now my dick feels like it's on fire, like somebody opened up my urethra and jammed in a habanera pepper. My hands are bloody waffles and now I might have an STD or some shit. I've got to sit down and just drown out the world until this trip ends.

I'm wondering if the e-bomb is going to accentuate my current pain as much as it used to accentuate the pleasure. I shiver, shove my hands into my pockets, and head back out, body on fire from the inside.

People are looking at me.

All of them.

Even the people with their eyes closed. I can feel it, waves of paranoia, sticking to me like molasses. The room smells like fried meat now, and aftershave. Mixed signals everywhere have me scared, twitching and tweeking. I spot the PartySmart table and stagger over, thinking I can ask them for help or something. The PartySmart group show up at the parties and try to encourage kids to abstain from drugs (or at least use them wisely), provide information on safer drug use, and offer free candy, and condoms, and other miscellaneous well intended services. As far as their actual effectiveness they are kind of the equivalent of a band-aid over a cancer sore. They don't do much, but it's nice to have them there. It looks better, PR wise.

At the table there are flyers with information about drugs I've never even heard of before, or maybe I've heard of them under different names. Blood of a Wig, Morning Glory Seeds, and Datura? What? Doesn't matter. Focus, come down, get help.

A kid with a blue goatee and a Rainbow Brite visor on sees me, and says something, but I can't understand what he says, through my panic. Sounds like maybe he said, "Treble morph de dealy whopper, man." It doesn't matter. Nothing else matters in light of what my eyes just focused on. I'm staring at the light blue flyer taped to the fake wood surfacing, and my heart is about to explode.

It's right there, and I touch it, real as day, I can feel the paper fibers, see the black ink lightly reflecting the pulse of a far off strobe. Too real, with bold print.

"WARNING-DO NOT PURCHASE DRUGS FROM THIS MAN. HE IS A KNOWN FELON, AND HAS SOLD HIGHLY DANGEROUS AND POTENTIALLY LETHAL DRUGS DURING AT LEAST THREE PARTIES IN THE LAST YEAR. HE IS A MEMBER OF THE NEO-NAZI GROUP KNOWN AS 'THE LIGHTNING REICH' WHICH HAS BEEN SPECIFICALLY TARGETING THE RAVE COMMUNITY FOR HATE CRIMES. IF YOU SEE THIS INDIVIDUAL PLEASE IMMEDIATELY ALERT LOCAL AUTHORITIES, OR LET SOMEONE AT PARTYSMART KNOW! THANKS, P.L.U.R."

Underneath the text, ugly as when I met him, is the one and only Stinky Christ, my chosen-at-random dealer for tonight's little get together. His name is apparently "Morton Greens," although that has to be an alias. I just can't imagine a Nazi I could call "Morty" for short. Less facial hair, but still definitely him, definitely, and I think I can smell him, even through the picture. I need to throw up, and the

PartySmart kid can tell something is wrong with me. I'm probably five shades of white right now, but I can't talk, I have to run away. To anywhere else. This is too real.

On the way into the main area I run into a door and my left hand leaves a smear of red, still oozing blood. I can feel the head of my dick, one hundred percent on fire now, like how I imagine a steam burn would feel, and I might be crying. Things are blurry, the music is too loud, too relentless. I'm confused, fumbling, trying to think about the Stinky Christ, trying to convince myself that I'm having a deeply bad trip and that in reality I'm probably just curled up in a corner somewhere, shaking, but the pain is too real, too sharp. How could that guy be a Nazi? He had so much hair! Nazis can't have hair! Shit, everything I'm trying to dig on is so blurry. Not a dream, my guts are fucking burning, really, incontrovertibly burning. I've eaten poison. My heart is going so fast now I can't even differentiate beats, panic through my whole chest.

Then I look around, and see hell, only this hell comes equipped with lasers, and strobes, and disco balls, and beats, which is all somehow much worse than a traditional fire and brimstone brand of hell.

Kids everywhere are doubled over; the one closest to me has a string of bloody vomit hanging from his lip. It looks like his little plastic necklace is sinking into his neck, scraping into his trachea. What did Stinky Christ a.k.a. "Morton Greens" feed us? Flashback on his joke, "...mutant streptococcus..."

NOT A JOKE! FUCKING SHIT!

My ankles roll out from under me. The floor is carpeted but I feel the concrete slap right into my skull. My skull gives too much, crusted red hands reach up and bring back new, wet blood. I can barely do it, but I shift my head across the ground, crane my neck, and see *him* behind the DJ booth.

It has to be him, fucking "Morton Greens", wearing an old World War II gas mask now, along with his hippie "camouflage", grabbing the live P.A. microphone. It's clear he wants to speak, but he seems to be having trouble finding the right switch with that mask on. I don't want to hear his voice, I just want a fucking ambulance, some help, anything.

Oh shit, "Morton Greens" found the switch.

The proud Aryan brothers of the Lightning Reich have a message to deliver to those of our race who seek to escape their duty...

What duty?! Fucking vapid Nazi bullshit, man! My head is throbbing, it feels thick, heavy, and loose on my neck, like if I move it any more my head will separate from my neck, accompanied by the sound of tearing paper.

Oh, God, please let me come out of this, I'm done tripping, done tripping, give me back control, fuck all these drugs, fuck Nazis and turntables and giant pants and stillborn relationships based on mutual drug abuse.

...to the Great White Crusade, to The Cause. Those of you before me this evening are suffering because you seek escape from the responsibility of our great brotherhood. You will die tonight because you chose to.

You will die tonight...

Fuck the candy kids with fake angel wings and candy jewelry and even all the beats. Fuck all this bullshit and give me back my life and take away this pain.

Let me wake up.

Nobody is listening. "Come on," I'm thinking, as I see security rushing around, as freaked out kids step over my body in a rush to the door, "I repent, man, let me come out of this." My head feels like it is burning now too, and I can't see anything anymore. I try to open my eyes. I have to see, have to crawl to help. I reach up gingerly to open my eyelids with my fingers and the tissue has too much give. Too much pain everywhere in my body, I didn't even feel my eyes rupture. They are soft in the sockets, like warm, wet, rotten little peaches. In my right eye socket my finger pushes up against the lens itself, hard yet yielding like a Superball, and now I feel the pain there...

...because you and your regressive and pagan behavior are contributing to the weakening of our race. The members of the Lightning Reich have decided that you race traitors have con-

tributed to our decline long enough. Now, we are cleaning up the mess, before the next generation is affected by your weakness, your ignorance, and your lack of desire for true societal advancement according to the rules laid out
by The Turner Diaries.
          Enjoy your last trip.

…and the top of my head is burning white hot, like an insanely *sharp* ache somehow, the whole head feeling rotten and close to caving with each throb, and "Morton Greens" seems to have stopped talking, and now I can hear screams, too many screams, too many of them pitched up ridiculously high, like the squeals and bleats of the slaughterhouse my aunt took me by when I was eight, and it feels like maybe my guts just spilled out, but I'm too afraid to reach down and feel, I just want to wake up, and I think God's a real bastard for allowing me to trip this hard, oh please let this all be a trip, and someone is screaming for their daddy across the room, and I want to cry but my eyes exploded so I just scream and scream and scream, and realize that the DJ likely ran from the building but he left the albums spinning, and I can feel the beats through the floor, vibrating my flesh and quickly rendering it into something less and less substantive, and I'm hoping now that if this is real I will die, and soon, and I'm also thinking, somewhere much further off, "Welcome to my After School Special," and I want to laugh, but my throat just dripped to the floor,

and

I

cannot

breathe.

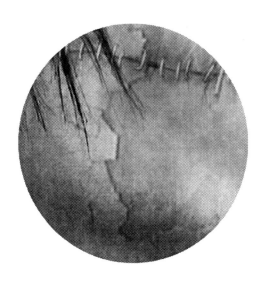

Passage

Of course, there's more to it than just that, than just the suffering, the screaming.

There are worse circles I could have shown you. Places where the physical doesn't even have a chance to manifest. Places with razor-filled wombs, acidic air.

Places with nothing at all.

I could have left you there.

But you did me that favor. You abandoned your friend at the door, and with quite a bit of gusto.

How did you know your fist would fit down his throat?

No response? That's okay. You've seen a lot today.

Best to remain quiet, even as we leave this place. You don't belong here with these charred remains. But mistakes have been made before. Quicksand seldom pushes people back up to the air.

So let's move quickly, eh?

This next place were headed to, it's almost as bad. Worse, in my opinion. Hope can be torture.

The people here, they think they've got a fucking chance to get out, to move up to the next level.

Sometimes I come here just to watch them. Just to laugh.

II. PURGE/DEEPER

1 deep

[mdma/dextromethorphan/methamphetamine]
and I'm still feeling everything (too much) and I'm waiting, with a
bitter taste at the back of my mouth like a whisper, its soft voice
promising *"Things will improve."* Tick tock tick tock tick tock... my
heart beat is faster, but good odds say it's psychosomatic (shit, if I
could get a psychosomatic high all the time I wouldn't need to eat this
poison every weekend; just a clean placebo buzz burning through my
system).

So the DJ bombs us with bass and everything is BOOM-
BOOM-BOOM-BOOM (God, it's got to be easy to produce trance,
house, techno, jungle, any of it, just turn on the drum machine and
strap a monkey to it, then hook that monkey up to an amphetamine
drip, teach it to twist knobs, tap buttons, nod head with meaning)
BOOM (no variety *please*, it might upset these regressive e-tards,
any kind of musical spontaneity might just overload the pill-addled,
pacifier-riddled waste around me, just keep it steady, straight and
thorough, four to the floor, whip these constant beats down this corri-
dor of escape, slap us into this sonic womb where the bass is so

maternal) BOOM-BOOM-BOOM and we submit to the barrage.

WITNESS THE AMAZING ANTI-SOCIAL ASSHOLE WHO BITCHES ENDLESSLY ABOUT THE NATURE OF HIS PEERS WHEN HE SHOULD JUST SHUT THE HELL UP OR GO SOMEWHERE ELSE!

Yeah, where is this bullshit cynicism coming from? This used to be fun, right? I ought to head for the chill room, find my girl, do something.

I'm going to need another

2 deep
[dextromethorphan/pma/pseudoephedrine/
guafenisin sulfate]
and I've found Mary talking to some guy who's like twice as big as me with a neck like a Goddamn telephone pole, who also happens to be dressed like an Abercrombie frat boy and I want to just pop him, but like I mentioned, the girth is in his corner, and I'm two pills into my evening, just waiting, hands gripping the wheel at the front of my cerebral cortex, ready for that ZOOM, BAM, BOOM, BADDA-BING kick off, the moment where my veins all fill up with sex and my eyes close over and do that

squiggle squiggle squiggle flutter leftright leftright leftright tremble/vibration shit that makes the world look like a perfume commercial, all soft and filtered and essentially perfect, but the pills have me agitated more than anything, so I grab her arm and spit,

"C'mon Mary!"

"Oh, hey Steve, hey, oh hey" and the eye contact from her is guilty for a split second, like maybe she was *too* interested in what this Frat boy had to say, and then she turns it on, the fucking beams, all green iris and dark pupil and long eyelashes and pouting lips and that smile like whiplash and I cave in, all the aggression gone (have my pills just kicked in?) and I'm kind of okay so,

"Who's your friend?"

"Oh, this is Dane. He's very sweet, he's a good soul."

Her pills have already kicked in. Once she's whacked

everyone is "sweet."

I picture it, sort of mad again, and she's saying to me, "Honey, this is John Wayne...what was you last name?" "Gacey." from the clown's blood red lips. "Oh yes," she sighs softly, "John Wayne Gacey. He's oh so very sweet, a real gentle creature."

Being innocent and naive and high all the time is about as safe as jogging next to the Grand Canyon with a blindfold on.

And people throwing rocks at you.

And strong winds pervading.

I say a little prayer for her every time we come to these "parties."

"Nice to meet you, Dane. Mary and I have some very important business to attend to somewhere else in the warehouse. Peace."

I grab her arm to pull her away and ask her why she's fucking with me, but there's instant resistance and Dane is puffing his chest out. I let the hand slide and turn away.

Bitches.

I need another

3 deep

[hydrobromide/dextromethorphan/baking soda/
methylcloroisothiazolinone/mdma]

...and I'm thinking, "Only at a party this wack, shitty, played out, etc. would I ever have to buy a dirty looking disco biscuit pill of specious content from some Ketamine-soaked, half-assed drug middleman who has no idea personally what's inside the pill that he just charged me twenty bucks for. He also apparently has no grasp on the fact that wearing glow-in-the-dark jewelry, a surgical mask, and a Scooby Doo backpack will never, ever, ever look cool, no matter how many drugs are ingested by the collective party consciousness."

HEY, OLD SPORT! MAYBE THIS GUY DOESN'T CARE ABOUT LOOKING COOL! MAYBE, JUST MAYBE, THIS GUY HAS A WAY FUCKED UP HOMELIFE WHERE POPS IS BASHING HIM ALL OVER THE HOUSE WHILE MOMS IS OFF

SCREWING THE ROTO-ROOTER MAN, AND ALL HE DOES DURING THE WEEK IS TRY TO LAY LOW, HEAL, AND HIDE! MAYBE THIS "BULLSHIT" IS HIS ONE WAY OF ESCAPE, HIS TINY, GLITTER SOAKED RELEASE THAT HE VISITS FOR JUST A COUPLE OF HOURS EVERY WEEKEND BEFORE HEAD-ING BACK TO HIS VARIATION ON THE DOMESTIC NIGHT-MARE! MAYBE THIS MUSIC, AND THESE DRUGS, AND HIS WEEKEND COSTUME, AND HIS WEEKEND PERSONALITY KEEP HIM FROM TAKING HIMSELF OUT HEMINGWAY GUTBLAST STYLE!

Yeah, yeah. Bored with it. My conscience. Hasn't said anything in my favor for a long time.

Where the hell did Mary go? I look back to where she was chatting it up with Dane the Suburban Neanderthal and spot nothing but empty carpet-space.

It's four in the ay em, I've eaten sixty dollars worth of ecstasy, and I can't find my girlfriend.

Fucked.

Quiet for a moment, thinking about loyalty until I realize that I'm three BOOM-BOOM pills BOOM down and the music the Music THE MUSIC(!) is sounding so good I just want to sink it into the base of my fucking skull and vibrate with it like that sequence in that one cartoon (the one with the replicating brooms) where all those strands of color start dancing around with the sonic waves, the red and the green and the blue all shimmering and smashing into each other and they like BOOM what the... oh ... oooooh *leftright leftright squiggle squiggle leftright* BOOM oh SHIT! and my one way flight to Highsville just blasted off at 747 speed so my brain is burning elec-tric and all I can do is listen and dance, pounding feet, pumping heart, and it's all so good, sososodamnright

just dance   just dance just dance faster

yes, this feels right just dance the music is

G.O.D. here

just

keep

moving

heart beat BOOM-BOOM please don't stop

it's all fucking   all of this is fucking

BOOM overandover BOOM-BOOM-BOOM

high

don't stop yes, so   (finally) keep dancing

replace my heart with a twelve inch polyurethane cone and turn up the

bass just BOOM-BOOM-BOOM-BOOM-BOOM overandover

head nodding, self approval and sweat dripping

burning.

just dancejustdancejustdancedancedancedancedance
        HEY, ISN'T YOUR HEART BEATING A LITTLE FAST!?
MAYBE YOU SHOULD RELAX, GET SOME WATER! DO YOU
FEEL OKAY!? WHAT WAS IN THOSE PILLS? WHERE'S YOUR
GIRLFRIEND?   WHAT'S YOUR GIRLFRIEND'S NAME?
WHERE'S DANE? WHAT ARE THEY DOING? WHAT DID YOU
EAT TONIGHT?
        ...fucking conscience.
        BOOM this is all too good, I don't feel like thinking about
myself ANYMORE!   (I don't feel like thinking).
        Escape.
        Where's that kid in the surgical mask, he's my brother now
and
        I need another

4 deep

[dextromethorphan]

What a riot, buying a pill from a fourteen year old girl wearing tin foil angel wings. Looked a bit like my little sister so I felt guilty for wanting to run my tongue down the crack of her ass.

YOU ARE LOW CLASS AND LOST, MY FRIEND! PLEASE GET SOME WATER! JUST ONE BOTTLE OF WATER AND I'LL BE QUIET! YOU ARE COOKING YOUR BRAIN! DON'T PUSH IT!

Oh, wait, don't move for a second and let my eyes re-orient themselves, I can't see straight and it's *leftright leftright leftright leftright leftright leftright leftright leftright leftright leftright* it won't stop now, I can't focus *leftright leftright leftright leftright leftright leftright leftright leftright leftright leftright leftright.*

I want to dance/I can't even see. No match up. Dysfunction. Lacking the proper means.

SUNBURST behind my eyes, FLASH like a punch to the skull, only it came from *inside* my head, and I want to throw up.

WHERE THE HELL IS MARY???????

I have to sit down (I feel five years old right now and I'm scared and I'm shaking).

So *hot*, just curl up, maybe someone will bring me water, I'm sweating so hard, I can feel it pooling at my lower back, dripping from my armpits, and I have to close up (pill bug, HA) and shut down for a little bit, and I close my eyes and thousands of crystal castles are being built and destroyed on the inside of my eyelids but it's not comforting or beautiful, it's not real at all, it's not the reason I came here (right?) and now I'm not dancing and *there's Mary* standing ten feet away and she doesn't see me and she's not alone and oh my God there's that frat boy and he's got his hand on her ass and she's kissing his neck like she used to kiss mine and I can't see where her hands are but one of her elbows is moving with a steady rhythm that breaks my heart and aren't they both so Goddamned sweet and healthy and why isn't she looking for me I'm right over here on the floor and there's another SUNBURST and my head, my head, my head oh

oh

oh

fuck

oh God forgive me.

I want to rest now.

{shutdown, stasis, near myocardial failure, distension of vessels proximal to the brain, fluctuating consciousness, regurgitation}

I HATE TO COME OFF AS A SELF-RIGHTEOUS CONSCIENCE HERE PAL, BUT YOU'VE NEARLY KILLED US TONIGHT SO I FEEL JUSTIFIED WHEN I SAY, "I TOLD YOU SO!"

shut up

Eight ay em in the morning.

Lonely, biologically toxic, near dead.

Smiling because I just found an accidentally discarded pill on the floor.

I open my mouth, close my mouth, swallow my poison escape route.

I step into the morning sun and pray that I burn today and shed these corrupted cells, this weak shell.

From the ashes, the million tiny phoenixes of my flesh,

pure and skybound.

Ascendance

This last place bothers me. Everything breaks down when you go inside.

Even you. You will collapse, but you'll see the rest of what you've been looking for. There are no explanations in there. Only an unfolding.

No pain, but no real joy either. It's almost nothing.

But it's a better kind of nothing than I could show you in the lower circles.

There's a weird hum to the place that makes my ears feel like they're bleeding.

Whatever you thought you knew, it'll melt down in there.

It'll liquefy and start humming. Vibrating. There's a sequence to it I can't peg, a rhythm under the buzz.

Listen to it, and maybe for once, the world will make sense.

Maybe, if you listen close, things will add up.

Maybe there's an answer in there.

What's that? Oh, "What's the question?" Well, not to go Zen on you here, but what *isn't* the question?

Clean the blood off your hands before you go.

Good luck in there…

III. TRANCE END/
A NUMBER OF THINGS COME
TO MIND

The Clearing At the End
4 Morning of August 23, 2002, 7:06am

When Quincy woke on the twenty-third of August in Our Year of the Lord 2002, his mind had been overcome with numbers. All he could think was one, two, three, over and over again. Those three numbers, the first we learn, the first things drawn in chalk after A, B, and C, were all Quincy had left in his mind, repeating in an endless loop, a mathematic mantra stuck in the skipping record of Quincy's gray matter. Quincy could not find a reason, or the will, or even the physical control to rise from his bed and greet the day. Quincy's mind had become the VCR that God never bothered to read the instructions to, flashing over and over in the dark. One, two, three, one, two, three, one, two, three, one, two, three, one, two, three...

The Path...

1 Morning of August 22, 2002, 12:31pm

12:31 will work. 12:32 will work. 12:33 has a Trinity in it, as in two plus one is three, and within the rules these two can be added since they are separated by the colon, and then the produced three is placed next to the two additional threes forming the digital Father, Son, and Holy Ghost. God in the numbers. You feel kind of pure if you rise when the alarm clock reads 12:33, like maybe if you let the Trinity into your head God won't fuck you up so bad this particular day. Good odds.

12:34 though, that's the winner. Sequential, one plus two is three, one plus three is four, and their reversals, and the whole batch adds up to ten, as in base ten, the foundation of our system, which put all these numbers in my brain in the first place. 12:34 is classic. Absolutely classic.

I watch the little digital figures realign, then 12:34, in all its perfection, is right there in my face, and I've got 60 seconds to roll myself out of bed before the less than ideal 12:35 clicks on and ruins my day.

I'm trapped in the shower for 48 minutes until 1:23 hits, allowing my exit. I occupy the time by memorizing shampoo ingredients (methylchlorisothiazolinone is a favorite, it's all prefix and has the same number of letters as the alphabet) and counting the holes in the shower head as the steam turns me pruny and leaves red streaks where the water courses down my shoulders, back, ass, and legs.

I stayed at my friend Chris' apartment two months ago and got "stuck" in the shower. I counted tiles for close to an hour, until his hot water became so frigid it sucked my breath down the drain with it. I emerged dead white and when he asked what took me so long the first thing that came to mind to respond with was, "Masturbation. I was masturbating. It was great!"

Keeping an obsession secret means "engaging in subterfuge." I prefer calling it that. Lying is haggard.

Lying is fucking necessary. Lying is the oil that keeps my duplicitous little lifestyle from overheating and turning into a grand and messy debacle. When you're an obsessive-compulsive, pill popping raver who works forty hours a week as a commercial loan analyst for a very reputable company, lying becomes your life's blood. I'd dry up and die without it, i.e.:

Do they have the credit to support that kind of debt?

Absolutely.

Are these e-bombs clean?

Clean as rocky mountain waters man.

So you'd recommend I avoid the annuities in favor of increased debt?

Ultimately, in this kind of tumultuous financial atmosphere, this kind of loan is the only sure thing. So yes, and I'm telling you this as a favor.

What'd you think of my set, dude?

Best fucking psy-trance, deep house, gay French happy hardcore combo I've ever heard. Fucking royal man. Plus you got the chicks fucking dripping for you man. The best. A-number-fucking-1 brilliant man!

The debt to income ratio seems a little rough. Can they afford this loan?

You have to look at the context on this one. Trust me, pigmy goats will outsell even the Bavarian grass-seed this year, it's a boom market.

Tell me it's not the pills. Will you tell me you really love me, baby?

Butterfly Jasmine Moonbeam, you are the most radiant, genuine, beautiful person I've ever met, and for me not to love you would be like asking God to reach down and pull my soul out and stomp it into a hundred ugly pieces. Of course I love you. Of course. Of course, of course, Oh God, OF COURSE! It's impossible not to love you, you have so much energy, and even though we've just met tonight, I know that for us to not share this energy would be a tragedy, and I'd regret it forever. In fact, I need to be closer to your energy right now.

What took you so long in the shower?

I was masturbating. It was great!

       Lies are the shortest way to reach one's goals, fulfill needs.

I'm not devious, just efficient.

Psychopath is a label.

My late afternoon breakfast is Cocoa Crunch. I eat 88 in-flated sugar puffs, eight per spoonful, eleven bites total. 88 works for me, and although I love the balance of the figure I always feel an unnecessary guilt in regards to the whole associative Nazi thing. The eighth letter of the alphabet is H. 88=HH. 88=Heil Hitler. My cereal consumption has no sublimated Hitler love in its pattern. 88 puffs fills me up. That's it.

The proper time rolls over on my watch and I'm out the door with my car keys jangling.

2 Afternoon of August 22, 2002, 2:34pm

As Quincy drove across the South Selby Bypass on his way to work his mind clouded over and familiarity navigated. His subcon-scious was at the steering wheel, his autonomic system was regulating each breath and beat, his conscious mind was barely registering the passage of time and space. Every day, five days a week, he spent an average of fourteen minutes on the road to work, barring unforeseen circumstances like auto wrecks, construction, or the sudden meta-morphosis of the pavement into a raging, great white shark filled ocean. This last circumstance was unlikely, but Quincy harbored the irratio-nal fear that the world could someday suddenly turn to liquid beneath him. In this liquid he knew *they* were waiting for him, the sharks, the great beasts, swimming in circles, staring black-eyed soulless stares at the surface, hungry, razor-sharp, and ready to consume him.

Solid pavement rushes underneath Quincy's car as he zones out to a near meditation level on the Bypass. The thirty two beat/four measure syncopation of Jungle music blasting from his speakers pulls his brain into a level of sedate stasis. The density of the sound, the constant nature of the beats, over and over and over again with very little change barring the occasional machine breakdown noise, all of this feels *right* to Quincy's brain. It matches his thought patterns, frantic and repetitious at the same time. One hundred and sixty beats per minute is Quincy's preferred tempo. Quincy has, on five separate occasions, had his heart beating at the exact same tempo for periods of time long enough to exhaust most hummingbirds. The third time this occurred Quincy suffered a severe case of "ratchet jaw" and nearly ground his teeth away. He could taste the enamel chips and tiny shreds of old fillings as he noshed away his face. As Quincy ground his teeth to the smoothness of river rock his brain was stuck repeating the alliteration, "Many milligrams of meth, many milligrams of meth..." The shady e-bombs he bought often contained more meth than trailer park ground water.

Quincy wakes up from his drive induced stupor just in time to park his Hyundai very attentively between the two faded yellow lines that indicate his spot at Sycorp Financing. Quincy loves the symmetry of a good parking job.

The next three hours find Quincy going through his motions. He processes, annotates, inquires, faxes, copies, designates, allocates, designs, aligns, contacts, files, piles, and manipulates. He twists numbers that represent weak income until they represent a sterling borrowing base. He smiles at co-workers and laughs at jokes without really listening to them. Quincy is not at work to interact. He is here because he loves numbers, and stability, and patterns, and dependability. He loves acronyms and tries to construct sentences out of them, which phonetically sound like gibberish. *We're gonna have to hepmar the roa if we don't want a deeker off the admin pee icey, right?*

As the right side of Quincy's brain tabulates fourteen months of collected gross income adjusted in relation to five years of projected annual overhead, the left side of Quincy's brain blackens. The blackness spreads in his mind, nulling and voiding what were once creative synaptic spaces, bits of colorful gray matter that lived outside of patterns and contained beauty and inspiration. The blackness spreads rapidly, like an ignited charcoal snake. The right side of Quincy's brain, where Quincy's soul had recently taken up residence in order to avoid the logicancer that ravished the left lobe, could not care less about the loss of the creative forces.

"Fuck it," Quincy thought rationally, "I've got a 401k."

"I've got my numbers," Quincy thought, and the part of his character that still resided in the atrophied wasteland of his creative mind caused him to break out in goosebumps.

After working a tiny bit of overtime Quincy gets ready to head home, already anticipating the ordered chaos of the night's rave in nearby Ellroy. As the clock clicks over to 6:23pm (reverse multipliers always work for Quincy) the automatic doors that open onto Sycorp Financing's foyer close behind him, and he's headed home.

3 Evening of August 22, 2002 11:11pm

Rats live on no evil star.

Picture, then, the virtuous star, swarming with vermin. Like this place. This fucking place is hip deep in vermin of homo sapiens appearance. The reverse palindromic logic plays out.

RADAR is the name of this party. Right now every element of the evening is soaked in palindromes, the time, the date, even the damn year, which is rare. I haven't been this excited about a year since 1991.

I arrived at the warehouse at 10:11 (a beautiful spoken sequential) and was greeted by the familiar sight of speaker towers, sacramentally lit DJ booths, and hundreds of bodies moving in mathematically precise patterns.

It's always the same at these raves, the same bodies, stuck in the same motions, the same minds locked into the same patterns of urge and abuse. It's just like my work, all process, no progress. We move in these patterns, we manipulate them, but we never force the answers out of them. I'm looking for something in the patterns, during my more hopeful moments. I'd say data catharsis, but that's not quite right.

Digital cleansing is closer.

When the acid hits me quick like this the connection speed goes way up. My brain is now running at 1,000,000 baud. The Lucy I bought from Mortis the Tortoise is racing through my brain like a power line dropped in a bucket of salt water.

A boy who appears to be about fifteen is standing to the right of me. He is nodding his head mechanically and holding his left hand over his heart. His right hand is stiff, fingers outstretched, and as he shuffles his feet with the music his hand traces the form of the cross from his head to his belly and then shoulder to shoulder. The Catholic raver is easy to spot. They swallow their MDMA communion and then wash over with guilt and serotonin at the same time. Thus, the rhythmic supplication.

The girl in the baby blue tank top to my left has made the same figure eight motion with her arms over two hundred times.

I'm not the only one stuck in these patterns. I'm aware of it, that's the difference.

I'm dancing listlessly to some boring four/four tech house, trying to get my brain deeper into its patterns, but it seems to be too simple. It's just one, two, three, four, one, two, three, four, over and over again, the least inventive drum pattern on Earth.

Bored. Four hits of acid deep and I'm bored.

I'm watching a golden frog make love to a gorgeous Aboriginal woman with purple eyes. This is happening on my left shoe. It's a worthless, meaning free visual, and I'm bored with it. This tech house is intolerable and the inevitable stink of rave sweat is bringing my dinner back up my throat for a second appearance.

Time to up the ante and try it. Time to give in to the temptation that always hits me at these parties. Time to exercise my affinity for all things Trinity, the big 3 x 3, tres squared, nine hits of liquid. Three threes, nine at once. If I can ingest nine hits of acid at one time, the Father, Son, and Holy Ghost will all jump behind my eyes and show me some pulsing, blinding, "tear it all down and restructure the fiber of reality in a new and superior way" type glory. The numbers work. Nothing beats the Trinity.

I've got the money for it. I do the footwork and spot my target, who appears to be selling some ecstasy to a family of four, two teens, a nervous dad, and a soccer mom.

Some say the rave scene has gone mainstream.

I wait for the Bradys to bail with their dope and then I make my transaction. Thirty dollars in Mortis the Tortoise's pocket later I've got a carefully dropped puddle of liquid Lucy in the palm of my left hand. Mortis thought I was crazy, but he's ultimately a capitalist, and has a hard time placing ethics or the safety of others above profit. So, he's got enough money to buy a couple of CD's and I've got enough acid to fry a herd of elephants.

I hesitate for twenty two seconds, pulse slamming with fear, the kind easily overcome by desire. Then I drop my face to my palm and quickly lap up my path to righteous digital cleansing.

3 x 3. A perfect triangle consuming my mind.

As if my act of faith had been rewarded the music slamming into us from the speakers speeds up and increases in density. The beats get faster and faster, grow closer and closer together, until they seem like dots forming a straight line of sound. I rush up to the front right speaker bank, and just as I get within two feet of the bass cones the interminable build crashes like a wave and a breakbeat almost knocks the air out of me. These piston driven speakers force the beats into my bones and vibrate my connective tissue. The sound is so thick here. I'm on the edge of a roaring forest fire, and for a moment I smell smoke. Then cotton candy, and I'm smelling it with every pore on my face, sucking in the smell through a million tiny mouths on the surface of my flesh.

"Oh fucking shit! Yeaaah!!!" someone screams to the right of me. My thoughts exactly. Jungle makes me feel like that, it contains ecstatic patterns, vortexes and sound-whorls. Being this close to the speakers gives me the sensation of being tossed around by a sonic tornado. The decibels are giving the mathematic and relentless jungle music substance, flesh. It is here to deliver us.

I stand erect in front of the speakers with my palms facing towards the sound, subject to it.

I close my eyes, and for one second I recognize the madness (123) of what I've done. There are thirteen total hits of acid doing God knows what in my brain right now. I have done this in pursuit of a vision, an escape. Part of me wants to run to the hospital right now and hook up a thorazine drip before this chemical roller coaster hits the drop.

I ingested the Trinity. It is too late.

I can feel the air from the bass impact cooling me in my ocean of acid-sweat, vibrating every tiny hair on my body. In my head it sounds like a high pitch whine is being run through a vocoder, getting louder and louder..

.eeeee...eeeeeeeeeeee...eeeeeeeeeeeeeeee...eeeeeeeeeeeeeeeeeeeeeeeeeeeeeeeeeee...

Then the doses hit at once and the world blurs thick in front of me like clear wax had just been poured into my eyes and when it washes away there are three trees in front of me dropping fruit and the fruit itself is made of crystals, millions of tiny, precise, and exact crystals, and I see people with no legs dragging themselves up to the trees and trying to bite into the fruit, which then whirls at blurring speed and shreds their faces into mists of bone and

"Oh shit! This dude's eyes are rolling back in his head. Dude, are..."

blood, and the blood gets pulled into the soil by these tiny blue veins that twitch like surfacing worms and grow thick with the blood of the legless people, whose bodies are decomposing into soft puddles, which are

"Rachel just ignore that. Some loady always has to fuck up the vibe, huh?"

themselves absorbed into the roots of the tree, and I look up from the ground and see these armless people walking in perfect circles around the tree, bellowing these low, threnodic moans, and some of them are staring at me, their eyes emptied of hope, and I'm trying to make sense of this when suddenly I'm looking at my hands, and they are moving without control, each

"Just fucking back up here people! He needs air. Somebody get the EMT..."

of them in front of me, tracing patterns that emit sound, like crystal humming, and I realize my hands are chasing each other along the infinite path of a Mobius Strip, and I feel something opening up in my head, and then I'm falling backwards and when I land and regain my footing I am

"..repeat, we are in transit to Mercy Central, we should arrive within..."

looking at two identical versions of myself, there are three of me in this small, black room, and I am inside each of us, all three of me (123), and we are pushing small wooden pegs into our hands, through the tissue, which welts around the wooden pegs until the surface can't bear the tension, and the peg pushes into our burst hands and numbers swirl out of the hole and rush up my arm and the numbers (123), millions of them, a vast legion of crawling

"...we need a chemstat CPC, and intubate him if he continues to..."

numbers are seething over our/my skin, eating away at it, chewing down to the bones, chewing in through my eyes to my brain, where they begin to circle, trapped, storming and then all I can see is a huge, dark orange sky

"Please restrain his arms, Peters, he could seriously harm himself if..."

swimming in numbers (123), and the pattern formed by the endless millions is pushing directly into me, into I, into my eye, which is perfect because eye is the name of the Trinity, Zeyeon, Eyesis, Oseyeris, I and Eye, three letters, each with three extensions when printed EYE, that perfect three at the center

"That's not possible. How can there be no brain signal at all? He's breathing."

of it all, every element of my existence has always been here in my mind, there is nowhere else worth being but here, God and eye are one, three in one, three in 1, 3 in 1, 3,2,1,1,1,1,...

1,2,3,1,2,3,1,2,3,1,2,3,

1,

2,

3

1

These numbers are all I ever needed. It is all I am.

I am 1ne.

2wo.

Thr3e.

AUTHOR'S NOTES

The League of Zeroes- When this story first appeared in Verbicide magazine, one of the accompanying illustrations featured the main character, onstage with his brain in a box, *wearing a crown of thorns*. This struck me as both unexpected and intriguing. I mean, this guy's not offering to absorb anybody's sins, but he's certainly gone through a lot of pain to be blindly worshipped by the television hoards, so he's got martyr status, I guess. But that assumed martyrdom shit would not fly in the Heartland. The guy would be off TV quicker than the exposed teat of a pedophile's sister.

Dissociative Skills- I was in the parking lot of the Lancaster Mall in Salem, Oregon, about to go over a speed bump in the parking lot, when this idea came to me: Guy gets high and guts himself for fun. Then I thought: You should not write this. So I wrote it that night.

Amniotic Shock in the Last Sacred Place- This story originally appeared in Pain and Other Petty Plots to Keep You in Stitches, a themed anthology centered on the hideous surgical art of acclaimed painter Alan M. Clark. In his "Pain Doctors" series of paintings a crew of cruel doctors experiment with human maladies and suffering in new and innovative ways. Knowing this may help you make more sense of the story. But probably not. There are two paintings that originally accompanied this story, "Terrible Infant" and "The Indifference of Heaven." You can see both of them, and more of the brilliant art work of Alan M. Clark, at www.alanclark.com

Precedents- Okay, I know the whole backwards thing has been done with Memento, and Irreversible, and Nas' song "Rewind," but this story just works better in reverse. You can, however, start at the end and read it from the bottom up to get a more traditional mystery, but you lose the emotional impact. I'm pretty proud of the murder method, too, since I'm a fan of closed-room mysteries.

Stanley's Lips- Based on an actual rock star who I find to be very alien in appearance. One of those guys who you look at and say, "Well, they had to become a rock star or else they'd never, ever get laid." He always reminds me of the way severe-vampire-Amy looked at the end of Fright Night, right before Ragsdale kills the main guy.

Snowfall- This is me on valium, trying to alleviate my own fear of impending nuclear disaster. The style is so much more sedate than my other stories, but for some reason this is a lot of people's favorite. It's pretty, I guess, if you're into that sort of thing.

Ex-Hale- I always watch the supposedly dead people in films. Tom Hanks flubbed his first feature film role by blinking after he'd been shot dead. And there's a very powerful scene in Mystic River that was pretty much ruined for me when I spotted the corpse taking some subtle breaths. You'd think they'd have learned to use prosthetics by now.

Working At Home- Hey, I was raised on Stephen King. And I'm obsessed with parasites. And Cronenberg. So now you've got this fairly traditional and ultimately nasty story of wormy body-horror. Keith Minnion did a great piece of cover artwork (one white wriggly worm perched on an eyelid above an open peeper) when this was originally the Featured Fiction in THE EDGE: Tales of Suspense.

Priapism- Manatees make me sad. The ending to this really bothers some people. Personally, I probably could have aced the father's "punishment" when I was fourteen, with no damage. Calling fourteen-year-old me "hormonally driven" is like calling Citizen Kane "slightly influential."

Luminary- I mainlined an ounce of crushed ants once, and briefly entered the "hive-mind." It turns out they mostly think about food, sex, and shelter. And strangely enough, dentistry. This is the only "nice" story I've ever written. It makes overly-sentimental people get misty, but I just like the imagery and Rockwell-meets-Twilight Zone tone of the thing.

Saturn's Game- C'mon, you know you've had thoughts like this guy. Someone once told me that there's no such thing as morality, and that it was just a social construct to eliminate a person's willingness to do hideous things. Or maybe I just made that up.

Branded- Deep social commentary about the invasion of corporate America into the fiber of our lives, or emotionally immature gross-out piece? You decide. Makes me feel downhearted, either way.

The Sharp Dressed Man At the End of the Line- I think that technically the quote goes, "There are two things that will survive a nuclear apocalypse: cockroaches and Cher." But the idea of having this fictional president walking around wearing Cher's skin just struck me as too unpleasant, even for this story. So you've got Twinkies, which I'm willing to wager also have a fair shot at survival. And as a side note, any avid James Ellroy fan can guess which of his books I read just a week before writing this.

Two Cages, One Moon- This is one of those ripped from the headlines pieces that I took and made into my own, only slightly weirder, story. And to people seeing some sort of childbirth metaphor with the nine-month-long kidnapping period in this story, stop looking so deep. What are you, fucking grad students? It was nine months in the real story. I kept it for my tale.

Sparklers Burning- Pour out a little liquor for M. Stewart, locked in the belly of the beast, making doilies with her new bitch Edna. For some reason I've always found arts and crafts materials sort of creepy. Do I owe Cronenberg for the momentary Videodrome imagery jack here? Yes, but don't tell him. He's vicious.

Last Thoughts Drifting Down- More nuclear terror, this time written under the influence of so many Mini-thins that I was literally dripping sweat while I wrote it. Ten points and a free book to the first person who can e-mail me at my website with the name of the famous scientist whose notorious quote is "hidden" here.

Swimming in the House of the Sea- Probably the most traditional "literary" story here, included because it's still fairly weird, and it's Chucky P.'s favorite. That guy knows what he's talking about, so the story stays in here despite the fact that no one dies, no one gets high, and nothing gets eviscerated.

Wall of Sound: A Movement in Three Parts- There's an homage to Dante's Divine Comedy here, but it's nebulous and set in the Northwest rave scene. These are fun for people like me who love reading about people on drugs doing fucked-up shit. Now I could throw the standard literary terms around, the ones critics always associate with drug fiction, like transgressive, subversive, anarchic, cathartic, etc. but the fact is, people like to read about other people doing drugs and committing crimes. Vicarious kicks are great, even if they're typically tempered by tragedy at the end of the tales. Thompson, Welsh, Selby, Frey, Ellis, Carroll… these guys have nailed it. I set this contribution at the base of that pantheon. I hope you enjoyed it.

ABOUT THE AUTHOR

Jeremy Robert Johnson is the author of Siren Promised (w/Alan M. Clark) and a multitude of acclaimed (and occasionally reviled) short stories, many of which are included in this collection. His fiction has been included in numerous anthologies and magazines and has twice been nominated for the Pushcart Prize. He is currently at work on a new novel.

He is not a coconut and refuses to believe so until you can provide empirical evidence to the contrary.

He currently resides in Portland, Oregon and operates a Private Investigation business under the name Shenanigans P. Doyle. So far his investigations have unearthed two facts: 1. He is not actually a detective. 2. He still believes, deep down in his heart, that one day Asia Argento will fall in love with him.

For more information, breakdancing advice, blog-esque materials, and news about upcoming projects check out:

www.jeremyrobertjohnson.com

ARTIST'S BIO

Morten Bak a.k.a. ketchup-suicide is a 24-year-old resident of Denmark (Copenhagen), and a multi-faceted artist whose work includes: cartoon concept/coloring, computer game character design/concept art/background art/coloring, freelance CD covers, book covers, and book illustration. Morten's ability to work in a variety of styles and media stem from his extensive art education, and his desire to create a look and feel to his dark art that is his alone. He credits the people around him, and the general craziness of the world, as great inspirations. He plans to spend 2005 bringing his often humorous, always dark vision to the worlds of illustration, and computer gaming art. To contact Morten, or to see more of his incredible work, you can visit: **www.ketchup-suicide.deviantart.com** or **www.artstar.dk**

ERASERHEAD PRESS

www.eraserheadpress.com

Books of the surreal, absurd, and utterly strange

WWW.AVANTPUNK.COM

A New Imprint From Eraserhead Press

BIZARRE NOVELS BY CARLTON MELLICK III

RAZOR WIRE PUBIC HAIR * STEEL BREAKFAST ERA
BABY JESUS BUTT PLUG * ELECTRIC JESUS CORPSE
SATAN BURGER * THE MENSTRUATING MALL
TEETH AND TONGUE LANDSCAPE * FISHY-FLESHED

9 780976 249832